Missing at Harmony Festival

Linda Tassel Mysteries Book 2

by Eileen Charbonneau

Print ISBNs
Amazon Print 9780228621720
LSI Print 9780228621737
B&N Print 9780228621744

BWL Publishing

Books we love to write .
Authors around the w.

http://bwlpublishing.ca

I0584510

Dedication

for Marya, our Georgia peach,
and Desmond, her California ray of sunshine

Chapter One

June, 1993

Shortstop Tad Gist eyed the man on second. Would he run? There was only one out. This was the Valdosta Valiants' last inning. He had to be ready.

Tad glanced up at the stands. He found Linda right away. She wore the red sundress that was his favorite. Her gleaming black hair stood out against the cloudless blue sky. She nodded. Yes, she agreed: the man on second would run on any hit.

The bat touched Joe's fastball. Bunt.

Joe was on it. He flung the ball to first. One out. First baseman Dave Neeley saw Tad tailing the runner. Throw, Dave, Tad thought at him. Do it now.

Dave hurled the ball. A great, calculated throw. Now, to be there to catch it and tag out the runner for a game-ending double play.

The afternoon sun was in Tad's eyes. His teammates would call him blind if he didn't make this catch. Blind bat from Buffalo, who can't take the Georgia sun.

Tad heard a thunk. He closed his mitt and kept running on the heels of the runner's desperate slide to third. They both went down.

Tad looked up through their dust cloud to see the umpire's puzzled face in an eerie, empty silence.

"Got that ball, son?" the ump asked.

Did he? Tad opened the glove without removing it from the runner's shin. There. A patch or white.

The umpire flicked his thumb over his shoulder. "He's out!" he bellowed.

Pandemonium erupted. Tad tried to find Linda in the stands, but his teammates descended, burying him under their cheers.

Maybe spending his senior year of high school in Atlanta hadn't been so bad after all, he decided as the Atlanta Andirons buried him in their embrace. Baseball helped. So had a change in attitude about his family's move. Tad had achieved that the summer before, with Linda's help.

Linda had come through again and again in the year since they worked together at the Mound Builders' dig site. She lived near the north Georgia site, two hours north of Atlanta. They'd only seen each other a few times over their senior year, but weekly phone calls and letters stuffed with photos and his little sister's drawings bridged the gaps.

Tad liked hearing about Linda's multigenerational household and her job categorizing the artifacts from the Mound Builders' dig they'd worked on together. He'd learned that Linda was a "bridge person"—one who pursued understanding between her Eastern Cherokee Nation and its surrounding Anglo culture. He admired her goals and empathized with her frustrations as she worked with the Cherokee council and the university on the artifacts' safe return after study.

They had common goals too—passing senior AP courses, applying to colleges, deciding on Morris University together.

Tad had never been involved with a girl like Linda Tassel. He wasn't even sure she was his girlfriend. He didn't ask her, because he didn't want to mess up what they had.

And now here she was, finally on his turf. But where? He had to find her. He struggled out of the grip of the dust and his team-mates' good will and pulled himself out of their circle.

The upper stands were empty. He felt cold suddenly, on that scorching June day. He shook off the strange feeling. Linda had gotten caught up in the swell of the Atlanta Andiron families and friends joining the players on the field, that's all.

She would be surrounded by her Cherokee entourage most of the time over the next three days, but he didn't care. He'd put up with all of them, even her clan brother, Guli Whitepath.

Her family had invited Tad to the Harmony Festival weekend in North Carolina, at the heart of the Eastern Cherokee Nation. When he'd met Linda last year, Tad didn't know anything about the Cherokee, past or present. All these months later he still felt like a novice learner, but he knew enough to be honored by the invitation.

Suddenly Maggie jumped into his arms. "Tad, you're all dirty!"

He hugged her. "Been playing hard, Sprite."

His little sister giggled and drew a lightening bolt through the smear of red Georgia clay on his cheek. Tad shifted her weight to one arm. She had just turned eight and was sprouting longer legs. More unwieldy, maybe, but she never felt heavy to him.

"Coach Kramer's direct quote? 'It was a wonderful end to a great season,'" his mother said in her best Kelsey Doyle, newscaster voice. "Nice catch and tag out, son," she added, grinning. "Can't wait to fill in your dad when he comes home from his conference."

Tad glanced behind his redheaded mother to the group of five Cherokee. The other families seemed to part around them, as if they were an island in their midst. He lifted his head higher and waved them over.

"That play was what the whole winning season was about, Mom—teamwork."

He said it because it was true, but also to please Linda and her friends. He'd learned from her that the Cherokee put a much higher value on community good than individual achievement.

Linda left the tight group and kissed his cheek. From her place in his arms, Maggie pulled her in closer. Little sisters can be very valuable, Tad thought, as he checked for her friends' reaction. The older man wore a grimace of disapproval, but the women were smiling. Guli Whitepath was not. He stepped forward and took the ball and glove from under Tad's arm. He fitted it to his own hand and threw the ball into the air twice.

"Too small," he said, and sniffed his disapproval.

Tad smiled. "I'll play with any size ball you choose, any game you choose."

"No handicap?"

"No."

Guli shrugged his powerful shoulders. "Maybe."

Linda snatched the glove from her clan brother's hand. She and Maggie rolled their eyes together.

"Boys!" Maggie groused, making everyone except Guli laugh.

Linda brought Tad into her group. "Ella Kituhwa and Ned Soco-wah, our festival chaperones, meet Tad, his sister Maggie, and their mother Kelsey Doyle."

Tad extended his hand toward the middle-aged man with sad eyes. He took it stiffly. Was he going to have to go through this guy and Guli to be able to see Linda alone? The girls lucked out with the woman, who was a study in contrast. As they made further introductions, her whole face danced in an inquisitive and mischievous way that reminded Tad of Linda's grandmother.

"I am Linda's cousin Ella, a niece of Delores Longknife," she said, explaining her resemblance.

Tad delved into his limited knowledge of the Cherokee language. "*Wa to*...for coming down here in time to see the game," he thanked them.

Ned looked over his head. "You are our guest. You will honor us at Harmony Festival," he said stiffly.

Linda brought Tad's attention to a smiling girl of about their own age. She matched the photos Linda had sent him of the two of them dancing together. "You must be Rising Fawn Reed?" Tad asked.

"Yes! You play very well, and run very fast."

Tad was surprised. Rising Fawn was pointing out his individual talents. Were her elders' eyes disapproving?

"Not fast enough against Linda's team at the dig last summer. I'm sure she told you that my stolen bases didn't go very far!"

"Can I touch your earrings?" Maggie asked from his arms.

Rising Fawn nodded, giggling as his sister's fingers sifted through the glass beads and porcupine quills. Rising Fawn was a little taller than Linda, with the same rich black hair, though she didn't wear it straight as Linda did. Hers cascaded over her shoulders in layered curls. Tad didn't know if the style was a perm or indicated the mixed heritage that many Cherokee shared, but he thought it was pretty.

He lowered Maggie to the ground.

"I'd better hit the showers so we can go. I'm looking forward to seeing you all dance at the festival."

As he yanked off his sweat-drenched uniform and stood under the steaming shower, Tad remembered his first meeting with Linda and their work together at the ancient dig site.

The job his father had gotten him on that first summer away from Buffalo had turned into an investigation after geologist

11

Michael Steffy was murdered and Guli arrested and under suspicion. Tad and Linda worked hard to clear her clan brother's name. They had succeeded, but only after almost becoming victims themselves.

Their summer had become part of the Cherokee oral storytelling tradition on the Snowbird reservation, Linda had informed him. Was his part in the story a good one, he'd asked. They wouldn't be inviting him to the Harmony Festival if they did not view him as a friend, she'd explained in her last letter. The festival was a community event, celebrated before the Smoky Mountain tourist season got underway.

Between last summer and Linda's few visits to Atlanta with her father delivering artifacts, Tad could only count their real "dates" on two hands. But he felt close to her. He went out with Julie Tolliver in Buffalo for a year. Since he'd last seen her, he'd received exactly one letter form Julie, full of wish-you-were-here events and parties.

Tad would never get used to Linda's chaperones, but he was determined to learn to accept them. Maybe Linda would never get used to Atlanta's faster pace once they started attending Morris University in the fall. Together. The prospect of college was less daunting knowing they'd be together. Linda was, Tad realized, his best friend. How had that happened?

"Hey, Gist, hand over the soap, if you're through dreaming about Pocahontas!" Mitch Ryder's voice pulled Tad out of his thoughts instantly.

Tad frowned at his team's catcher, but passed him the soap without a rejoinder. He'd given up talking to any of them about Linda. Even the ones who might understand would be overruled by Mitch's big mouth.

Which continued. "Going to her pow-wow instead of our graduation party, is what I hear. Now I call that un-American."

"It's not a pow-wow," Tad said evenly. He yanked the shower handles down and toweled off quickly. "And it's more American than anything you'll be doing."

Mitch followed. "What does a Polack-Mick know about being American? We Ryders have been in this country since—"

"Since the first Americans were watching from the shore," Tad finished for him.

"The professor's got you these, Mitch," Joe Neeley said affably, coming between Tad and the catcher as both finished getting into their T-shirts and jeans.

Mitch pushed him aside. "Sure, no use us pea brains talking to the big-time archeologist's kid."

"My father's an anthropologist," Tad said quietly.

"That's right. Your daddy studies monkeys looking for the missing link, right? That's why he hangs around Indians and n—"

"You're way out of line, Mitch," Joe said, blocking Tad's path to him.

"What are you going to do, Polack?" Mitch challenged him now, "Slip her big brother a bottle of Thunderbird to get him off guard duty?"

Tad's thinking stopped. Blind rage took over. He pushed past Joe Neeley. But his punch was off, and too expected. It glanced off Mitch Ryder's jaw. The catcher grinned as he kneed Tad in the gut. When Tad stumbled, Ryder slammed him with a hard right. Tad tasted blood. He swung out wildly but it was all over. Coach Kramer stood between them.

"You've been trying my patience all season, Ryder," he yelled. "So careful to keep yourself within an inch of getting thrown off the team."

"Gist threw the first punch, coach! Ask anybody!"

"Get inside."

The coach only shook his head in Tad's direction, then followed Mitch Ryder into his office.

Tad wiped the side of his mouth. Great, he thought. Trying to punch his way out of an argument with the school's top jock. A perfect way to start Harmony Weekend. He hoped the Snowbird Cherokee were more tolerant, or less strong. This could get old.

Tad finished dressing, threw his uniform and the rest of the contents of his locker into his duffle bag, and tried to get past the coach's office unnoticed.

Not a chance.

"Gist. Your turn."

Well, at least his antagonist had gone, leaving a trail of Calvin Klein Escape cologne in his wake.

"Sit."

Tad entered his just-the-essentials office and sat in the plastic chair beside the lanky coach's desk. Coach Kramer threw a packet of blue ice at him. Tad dutifully placed it over his cut lip.

"I did throw the first punch, sir."

"I know that. Also heard what came before, the end of it, anyway. And other times, ever since your girl came to our first game in April. Let's see." He lifted the blue ice packet. "Better," he decided. "Don't want her showing her people the punched-out ball-player she's chosen, do we?"

"No, sir."

His coach tossed the ice packet back in its cooler. "Go on now, son."

"That's all?"

"What do you want? A boo-boo cover?"

Tad jumped from the chair and headed down the empty corridor.

"Gist?"

He turned.

"Be careful up there. That Snowbird Cherokee Softball team plays hard. Fair, but hard. I played them in the sectionals. Give my regards to Stoker Vann. I expect you'll meet. Mean fastball. Don't swing unless it's a clear strike from him, hear?"

"Yes, coach. Thanks. Not just for today. For the whole season."

"Uh, about that last play. I didn't know if you had the ball or not. Did you?"

Tad grinned despite the pain it caused at his lip. "Nope. Neither did the ump. Guess we all found out together, coach."

Chapter Two

Linda touched Tad's bruised lip. When did that happen, she wondered. "That was quite a slide, Buffalo Man," she said, using the name she'd given him back at the Mound Builders' dig.

"Yeah, well, we all played hard." He turned away from her scrutiny, wincing. It didn't do him any good to hide from her, because he ran into his mother.

"Tad."

"Coach iced it, Mom."

Linda watched his pale skin redden. Poor Tad. She'd often teased him about his face's inability to hide or evade a truth. He had not gotten that bruised cut during the game. His mother knew it too. He'd been fighting, she figured. With that boy, the team's catcher, who always sneered at her, who also came out of the locker room later than all the others.

Tad walked past them both to her friends. He addressed Ned Socowah.

"Sorry to keep you waiting. Should we get going? Those mountain roads after dark might be tricky."

Ned frowned. "We know the way."

"Sure, of course."

His blush deepened. Poor Tad. His mother came to his rescue, lifting the wicker basket at her feet and took Maggie's hand. "We'll walk you to the van. Linda, Rising Fawn—may we have a peek at your costumes before you go?"

"Sure." Linda smiled at Tad's mother, ignoring the deepening frowns of the men.

Cousin Ella came to her rescue. "Our dancing clothes are called regalia." she explained gently. "They reflect our traditions as well as our lives, interests, and family background."

"We wear them with responsibility and pride," Ned added.

"Regalia," Kelsey repeated. "How wonderful."

Good. Now they were all smiling, even Guli.

In her looks, Kelsey Doyle was as far away from a traditional Cherokee woman as anyone could get, but Linda always felt a kinship with the flame-haired woman. Perhaps it was based in that curiosity and childlike wonder that she shared with both her children. As they walked, her younger child, Maggie, took Rising Fawn's hand.

"How did you get your name?" she asked.

"My father named me when I was very little. He said that's what I looked like as I was trying to walk."

"Like Bambi on the ice?"

"Yes."

"You walk fine now."

"Thank you."

"And you dance?"

"We all dance."

Maggie took both Linda and Rising Fawn's hands and swung them as they walked. She lowered her voice. "Even him?" She nodded in Guli's direction.

"Oh yes," Linda said. "Rising Fawn and I dance with our shawls, Guli with his hoops. We are all butterflies."

"What do you mean?"

"We will show you."

The men brought the pack box down from the van's rooftop and opened it. The clear plastic bags holding their regalia were on top. Kelsey Doyle's eyes were almost as wide with interest as her daughter's. Ned and Ella could see that, surely. They would know that Linda had made a good choice in inviting her friend Tad to Harmony Festival. No matter how different he was from her beloved *Tsa la ki*, the Cherokee, he came from good people, too.

Maggie's small fingers reached for the dyed gold deerskin of the shawls as Cousin Ella told the story of the dance.

"The girls represent the women who have lost their warrior husbands in battle."

"How sad!" Maggie exclaimed.

"Yes," Ella agreed. "At the beginning of the dance, the widows go into their cocoons in grief. They cry beside the Lake of the Wounded."

"Where?"

"It is a place deep in the Smoky Mountains. A place that only a few are privileged to see. The women go there, in their cocoons, and the spirits of their husbands rise up from the lake."

Linda watched Maggie tug tentatively on Guli's sleeve. "That's you? The warriors' spirit?"

"Yes. I can be anything with my hoops—eagle, snake, butterfly."

Linda looked to Rising Fawn and smiled together. Little Maggie was getting Guli to talk of dancing, the passion of his heart.

Ned, a marine vet who helped inspire them to create the dance, now crouched beside the little girl and her mother. "The warriors' spirits rise, and the women..." He hesitated, cleared his throat, but couldn't seem to continue.

Cousin Ella touched his arm. "Are turned into butterflies," she finished for him. "They are free to start a new life. Linda, who we call—"

"Ahyoka!" Maggie said.

Ella smiled. "Exactly. Ahyoka is the wild rose butterfly, and Rising Fawn is the Maple Leaf Butterfly—see the patterns on their shawls?"

Rising Fawn unzipped their bags and ran Maggie's fingers over the shimmering beadwork pattern of their shawls...deep pinks and greens in Linda's and bursting golds and oranges in that of her friend. Maggie sifted through the garments' long fringes.

"They're so beautiful," the little girl said wistfully.

"Theirs is a dawn dance on Sunday, before the softball game. You are invited to both."

Maggie looked up at her mother, who nodded. "We will leave early to pick up Tad," she promised. And son," she turned to Tad. "Here's a graduation present so you can keep all your commitments this weekend."

Kelsey Doyle slipped a long box from her handbag and gave it to Tad. Linda watched her friend's eyes spark with delight as he opened his mother's gift.

"Wow, Mom! The Fossil ® I was admiring! The one I liked best!"

Linda came closer. "Fossil ® ?" she asked, perplexed.

Tad laughed. "It's not a petrified remain, Linda. It's the brand name of a watch. Look," he invited, placing the opened box in her hand. Its woven leather band was handsome, but the face of the watch fascinated her most. It was so large it might span her own wrist. And it was the dark blue of a clear summer night in the mountains. Inside a carved-out half circle between the hours of ten and two, there were glittering stars and a moon coming up over the horizon.

"They glow in the dark," Tad told her, "and you can set it like an alarm clock, or use it as a timer."

"I think it is very fine," she said, before passing the time piece to the rest of her party. They all made approving noises except for Guli, who rolled his eyes.

Linda had trouble with white people's exact measurement of time. On one of her visits to Atlanta, she toured the television news place where Kelsey Doyle worked, surrounded by clocks that told the time of every place in the world. Her father had not worn a watch since he'd married her mother and come to live among the Cherokee. But James Tassel taught Linda that it was necessary to be punctual for her appointments in the world outside. He had not forgotten that part of being a white man. Maybe he could explain why Kelsey Doyle thought Tad needed her gift at Harmony Festival.

The van's first stop was at a gas station and park-like rest area just outside Atlanta's Perimeter Highway. Linda got out of the vehicle and glanced over to where Guli and

Tad were talking. Arguing, was what it looked like—about baseball versus softball? Ned stood apart, skimming stones across a small brook near the picnic tables.

People remembered Ned as a happier man. He lived alone in his cabin since he'd retired from his military service. People said he had studied chemistry and had dangerous work with explosives and solvents when in the marines. Maybe they poisoned him, the stories said. That's why he lived alone, to regain his balance in the natural world of the mountains.

He could only be coaxed down for ceremonies and festivals, or if anyone was in need of healing roots and herbs of the higher altitudes. Linda remembered his soothing words as he pressed plantain leaves against her cut knee hen she was a child. He did not look troubled then.

"Why did Ned need you to tell the rest of the story of our Butterfly dance?" she asked her cousin as the women walked together.

"It put his sister into his mind, maybe," Ella said.

Linda remembered. Right before the Aurora Toy Factory on reservation land closed down that past winter, Ned's younger sister had lost her husband to an accident there.

"Is Shirley not doing well?"

"She has the fading sickness. Ned took her into his cabin a few weeks ago, hoping his company might help. But it's lonely up there."

It was as close to a criticism of the idea as her gentle cousin would come, Linda realized.

Linda watched Ned stop throwing stones, say something to Guli, then head for the stop's pay phone, fishing into his pockets for change as he walked.

Rising Fawn nodded. "No: *kwa!*" she breathed out. I think, your cousin, she speaks to the sacred people of the mountain, Linda!" she teased.

Linda elbowed her dancing partner playfully. "And the sky people listen to her wisdom, and tell Ned to ease his sister's loneliness by phoning her?"

Their chaperone smiled. "Perhaps he eases his own worry. Come, you two magpies, let's get back on the road. There's a long journey ahead."

"What are these?" Guli asked Tad, like a challenge.

"My mother's cheese balls."

Guli took a tentative bite.

"Well? How does it taste?"

"Different."

"Different good or different bad?"

"I'm still deciding," he said, reaching for another.

24

Rising Fawn, in the van's third row seat beside Guli, swatted his arm playfully. "Pay no mind to his words, Tad. Count how many he's eaten!"

Linda watched Cousin Ella turn around from her front seat.

"Please tell your mother our entire supper was delicious, and we thank her."

"Be glad to, Mrs. Kituhwa."

Guli grunted. "Bread's good."

"That's Irish oat bread," Tad told him. The sausage is Polish—called kielbasa."

Linda laughed. "Your sister Maggie was very kind to write my name on the wrapping of the most generous portion, Tad. She must have remembered how much I enjoyed it over my spring visit."

Guli leaned forward, looking with concern to where a driving rain was now pelting the front windshield of the van. "Highroad might be flooded," he warned Ned. "Be careful outside Elijay."

Linda appreciated her clan brother's observation skills and knowledge of the roads. She loved his surefooted dancing with its contortionist-like moves, too. If only he didn't keep Tad so occupied with challenges and arguments. It was like having another chaperone.

Guli was only a little older than she and Tad were. Couldn't he understand and give them more breathing room? Linda was sure that Tad was so concerned about earning the Principle People's trust that he might not even ask to kiss her over the Harmony Festival weekend. It had been months since their last kiss. This would be hard to bear.

The night before she had been so excited about the trip that she drew up a list when she couldn't sleep. "The Agonies and Ecstasies of the Long-Distance Boyfriend" she'd named it. The list had a plus and minus column. No touching over the telephone wires was a minus, but was offset by wonderful letters. Hardly ever fighting with him was great, hardly ever seeing him was not. Treasuring each other was beautiful, but was that beauty real, or a ghost they had built up in their longing, their imaginations?

Linda leaned back in her seat and tried to stare out through the windshield wipers' monotonous squeak. The rainfall was intensifying, thunder and lightening coming closer together. She felt a whisper of warmth first, then caught Tad's summer scent: the leather of his baseball glove and that pinewoods soap he used. She felt her heart beat faster. How she loved having him close.

Linda remembered his scent from last year, at their time at the Mound Builders' Dig. The wonder of him was not her imagination. She knew this boy had a fine courage in him. Their friendship had tested that courage. She could trust him with her life.

Under the red folds of her sundress, Linda felt one, then another, of his fingers touch hers. Slowly, as when she wanted to watch a deer approach the salt lick behind her house, she shifted her gaze from the windshield to Tad.

Even on this moonless, starless night, even on this dark mountain road, she could see glints from his gold hair. His blue eyes picked up a reflection too. From where? The dashboard's lights? This is a *vo: wa ne: ka*— a white person. Very white. He would not be welcome on a night hunt with her ancestors. Those light eyes and hair would frighten the night animals. But here, now, in front of two chaperones and her dancing partners, Linda wished she had the courage to tell Tad Gist how happy looking at him made her feel.

He smiled. Even his teeth shone. Linda remembered that Tad had Irish heritage. So did her own father. Her father said that part of Tad maybe allowed him to have visions, like the one that warned him there was danger at the dig site.

Could he read her thoughts?

She felt herself grow warm and turned her attention back to the storm. Just in time to see a tree limb come crashing down before the headlights.

"Ned—stop!" she cried out.

Chapter Three

Tad felt suspended in mid air. It was exciting for the fraction of time when it felt like flying. Then he realized that the van was hydroplaning. He tucked Linda's head under his arm. He heard crunching metal, breaking glass. Then silence, except for the rain, and spinning wheels.

He looked under his arm. No one was there.

"Linda?"

"Coming." The click of her seatbelt, and she fell with a thud into his arms.

"Sorry."

"I'm not. You feel great."

She laughed into his chest. "Can you reach the door handle?"

He searched through the darkness.

"Above us. The van landed on its side," she directed him.

"Right." He released his seat belt. His feet found his mother's sturdy picnic basket and stepped on top. He unlocked, then opened the sliding side door and lifted himself out.

A flash of lightning illuminated the inside and movements. Linda had somehow found a flashlight and was gently calling the names of the other passengers. They all answered with only Mrs. Kituhwa's voice edged with pain.

"Let's get you out first, Cousin Ella," Linda said, coaxing her kinswoman out of the front passenger side. "Don't worry, Tad will be waiting, won't you, Tad?"

"Sure. I'm right here, Ma'am." He anchored his feet, ready to lift the small woman.

"It's not bad, a pulled muscle maybe," she said, smiling up at him.

"Take your time," Ned Socowah said from the driver's seat in the darkness of the van. Tad only saw his hand as he passed Cousin Ella to Linda who helped her rise to Tad's waiting arms.

The small woman was not heavy at all. Tad hoisted her until she was sitting beside him. Then he eased her to the ground.

"Rising Fawn's ready," Linda called.

"Anything hurting?" Tad asked Linda's friend.

"No. It is Guli who got struck with my elbow in his ribs."

Guli grunted. "It would take all four of you to do me any damage."

Tad pulled a nimbler Rising Fawn out of the van. She stood beside her chaperone on the muddy shoulder of the road. With her curls plastered down by the rain, her hair looked more like Linda's.

29

The van rocked a little when Guli stood. Waving away Tad's arm, he tried to climb out by himself twice. Then he took Tad's grip and succeeded.

Tad sniffed the air inside the van.

"Yes, gasoline," Ned Socowah confirmed from the darkness. Then his voice sounded strange. "I have to call my sister."

Linda found him with her flashlight. "Yes, sir. We can walk down the road to that motel we passed, remember? You can call her from there. Let's get you out."

Guli touched Tad's sleeve. "One of us, under each arm," he suggested.

Tad nodded in agreement.

They made contact and heaved. Ned Socowah came up unevenly between them, Guli's greater strength causing the lopsidedness. But Ned was soon standing on his own with the others.

Only Linda was left.

"Do not use that method," Rising Fawn warned them. "She's too small to be your wishbone."

Tad saw a glimmer of amusement in Guli's eyes. But when they turned together they saw that Linda was already out of the van. She reached for each of their hands before she jumped to the ground.

They all did a quick examination of each other with the help of Linda's flashlight and found a few bruises and bumps besides Ella Kituhwa's hurt arm. Linda removed her head kerchief and made a sling for her elder's arm. Then she touched Tad's sore lip. Her cold finders felt good on his cut.

"Now we all look like we have been fighting," she said.

"Fighting?" he asked.

Lame. She knew, of course, about his altercation in the locker room. She gave him that frown he'd seen before—scowling, but with enough amusement to know he'd already been forgiven.

"Is the top box crushed?" she asked then.

It was intact. Together, all but Mrs. Socowah released it from the van's roof and dragged it under a sheltering tree.

They met no traffic as they trudged their way back to the road-side motel, The Knotty Pine Haven. Its small log cabin windows had shutters stenciled with the outline of pine trees. Tad led them all into the one-story building that was the office. Then he volunteered to stay outside on the road with the flashlight to warn cars of the downed tree limb head that had driven their van off the road.

The impact of the crash finally hit him then, as he stood in the rain, shivering. They were safe, they were all safe, he kept telling himself, but he could not make his shaking hands stay still. He concentrated on figuring what he could do to stop a car and keep what had happened to them from happening to another group of travelers. The concentrating helped, along with Linda joining him, easing the flashlight from his hand and slipping the slick yellow poncho over his shoulders.

One of the motel managers, a tall guy with a handlebar mustache, was with her to take over Tad's roadside duty and set out flares.

"I'll bring more up the road at the accident site. Go in now, youngsters," he urged.

As they walked up the short woodland path that he directed, Tad eased the final trembling from his fingers in the warmth of Linda's hand.

"Everyone here is so kind, Tad," she told him. "When they heard we were part of Harmony Festival, they insisted we stay the night at two of their tourist cabins. Guli tried to thank them with the gift of his best silver ring, but they wouldn't hear of it. They never miss his dancing at the festival, they said. And they'll haul our box up here in their truck. Imagine! We can get warm and dry and even get some sleep and then still—"

"Linda?"

"Yes?"

"Everyone's all right?"

"Yes. How about you, Buffalo Man?"

"Good. I'm good. But, when I was alone, with the flashlight on the road. I guess my mind started racing. And I couldn't keep my hands from shaking."

Linda smiled. "Mine, too, when I was signing the guest register for us. And I have been talking like Magpie, while you can hardly speak at all! Funny, huh?"

"You were wonderful," he said quietly.

"So were you. I guess we did all right, when we had to."

A flash of lightning let him see her smile.

As they got closer, Ted spotted Ned Socowah by a small cabin's porch, peering into the darkness. He hadn't seen them yet. Tad drew Linda behind the trunk of a young pine. He liked the strength of her hand at his shoulder. And the way the rain made her dress cling to her shape. They were probably not to be this close, in the dark, but her polished stone eyes said she didn't mind.

"We're so lucky, aren't we?" he whispered at her ear.

"Yes." She hugged him hard, burying her head against his heart.

"*Ky: ke: yu*?." he said words that she's taught him. Because life was too precious to not talk about important things.

"And I love you, Taddeusz," she answered.

Tad kissed the top of her rain-scented hair, then her temple, then her waiting, open mouth. She tasted like raspberries.

"Linda! Tad!" Ned Socowah called out, as though they were lost in the deep woods.

"Ahyoka!" Cousin Ella tried Linda's Cherokee name from where she stood on the second cabin's small porch. "Did you find him?"

Linda buried her head in Tad's chest again and laughed softly. "Do you mind them?" she asked.

Tad smiled. "I'd better mind them, if I have any hope of being alone with you again."

Linda raised her head. "Yes, Cousin, I found him!" she called back.

"Well, bring him in out of the cold."

Tad squeezed Linda's small waist between his hands. "I'm not cold, Mrs. K!" he insisted.

Linda swatted his shoulder, breaking his hold, before yanking him from the shadow of the tree.

Chapter Four

Rising Fawn came into their small bedroom of the cabin, wrapping a fluffy white towel around her head.

"We don't even have to walk to the showers here, Linda!" she marveled. "What a wonderful place."

"Yes," Linda agreed.

Her friend bounced on the room's double bed. "Not so wonderful to you, maybe? You have been to Atlanta. To Tad's house," she nodded toward the door that led to Ella's bedroom, "Without chaperones."

Linda sat cross-legged. "I have visited his whole family. And little sisters are very good chaperones."

They laughed together until Rising Fawn lifted her head, then went to the small front window and lifted its green gingham curtain. "I thought I heard someone."

"This is a motel. There will be more people around us."

Her friend dropped the curtain and crossed her eyes at Linda. "Yes, City Girl."

"I am not a—"

Rising Fawn giggled. "Tad is nice, just as you said. And so brave. I like him. Looks are not everything, are they?"

"What is the matter with the way he looks?"

"Nothing, nothing!" Rising Fawn removed the towel from her damp hair. Her permed curls sprang to life under her crushing fingertips. "Is he very rich?"

"Stop changing the subject. Now, what is wrong with—"

"He must be rich. His mother is a TV star."

"She is a news reporter."

"On TV. Like Connie Chung!"

"Not like Connie Chung. Kelsey Doyle is on the Atlanta news only. She is not paid the same salary as Connie Chung."

"She is beautiful. Tad must look like his professor father then, eh?"

Linda flung a pillow at her friend, who made an exaggerated "oof" sound and crumpled. "Oh, stop tormenting me, Ahyoka, she pleaded, before her voice went quiet. "Because I love an A *o: wa nee: ka* too."

Linda sat closer to her friend. "Who?"

"His name is Jim Greene. He lives on Fontana Lake. He gave me this."

Rising Fawn revealed a necklace that was tucked inside the flowing nightgown she wore. It was a silver intertwining rope design, delicate and beautiful.

"After our accident, when the van went over and we all got out, safe, my first thought was to reach for it. If everything else we brought had tumbled down the mountainside, I would not have cared. As long as I still wore the necklace. Thant was when I knew I love Jim Greene. Ahyoka, let me comb your hair, my hands are shaking. This is the first time I have told anyone, even myself."

"You honor me," Linda said quietly, handing her friend her comb. She turned, and soon felt Rising Fawn's gentle touch as she guided the comb through her own freshly washed hair.

"Where did you meet?"

"At Shirley Cutcheon's house. I was visiting her on that terrible day the men came to tell Shirley about the one who is gone," Rising Fawn began, careful not to mention Bobby Cutcheon, Shirley's dead husband. It was not polite to name the dead. "Jim Greene was his best friend. Well, maybe his best white friend," she amended, her head tilting to the men's cabin, where Shirley's brother Ned was sleeping." They both won scholarships to the training school the Aurora factory sponsored for promising students. Jim is now twenty-two and is floor manager and owns his own trailer there on the lake where the herons nest."

Linda glanced at the reflection of her friend in the room's mirrored dresser and watched her wide smile fade. "Jim tried so hard to save the one we lost, after the accident at the factory."

"The other man who came that day to Shirley's house, he was the boss of them both. He did not like being there, I think, watching us cry, because he left us. Oh, Linda, your hair looks like a midnight waterfall. Shall I braid a few plaits in it?"

"Yes, please." Her friend's voice was so soothing in this place far away from home. And she wanted to hear more of her story. "Did Jim Greene stay with you and Shirley?" she prompted.

"Yes. He spoke so softly, saying he had seen us both when our Church of the Dove choir visited around the town at Christmas and festival times. He said he loved our music. He held Shirley's hands and answered all her questions, even about the blood and pain. Most white people are not like that, my father says. They are stingy, even with grief. They run away, like the factory boss did that day. But Jim stayed with us, even though his own eyes were full of sorrow.

"Jim came back on his motorcycle on each of the three days the family was contaminated by death. He has a black and

38

red Yamaha ®. It rides like the wind. He came for the funeral and the burying, even though his boss told him not to say that he was sorry, because then Shirley might sue the factory. My father even shook Jim's hand."

Linda's eyes widened. "Your father does not yet shake my father's hand." Few of the Snowbird Cherokee did not accept and respect James Tassel enough to shake his hand, but Swimmer Reed was among them.

Rising Fawn's plaiting finders paused. "This is true, to my mother's and my sorrow. Do you know this?" she asked.

"Yes," Linda assured her friend.

Rising Fawn tied off the braid and began another. "After, Jim came back. Not to visit. At first he left things on our doorstep."

"What things?"

"A sack of apples, a pot holder he made, wildflowers from the lakeside. I listened for the sound of his motorcycle and met him at the door. We talked. He would ask me about school, the choir, my dancing with you and Guli and how Ned helped us find meaning in our steps and formations. He would tell me about his work, and layoffs at the factory, and how beautiful his spot on the lake was. After Jim left, I asked my father if we could invite him in. Again and again. He always said no.

"'Who is the stingy one now?' I told my father. It was a bad thing to say Ahyoka, I know. I said it in anger. My father hit me in his anger, too, I know that. But after that, I ran toward the sound of the motorcycle, and got on it with Jim, and buried my tears in his back."

Linda turned and took her friend into her arms. "You have been seeing each other since then?"

"In secret, yes."

"Is he good to you?"

"Oh yes! Good, and kind and respectful. He asks before we kiss, does Tad do that?"

"He does."

"Jim did not turn mean or start drinking even after the factory closed, and he had no job. He says there is work in Marysville, over in Tennessee. If he gets this work, he wants to sell the trailer. He wants me to marry him, Ahyoka and go away with him."

Linda squeezed her friend's fingers between hers. How had Rising Fawn grown up so fast? How was she already a woman? Her friend thought Linda worldly and mature, because her family no longer lived on the Snowbird reservation, because she had been to Atlanta. But Rising Fawn was the one thinking of marriage when she was yet to turn nineteen.

"Do you want this man?" she asked her friend.

"Oh, yes! But I don't know what to do. My father goes on with the dances, and the church, and his plans for me to stay on Snowbird land. Jim sees us in this silver necklace, bound with each other through our lives. I am not my father's little dancer any more, Ahyoka. But am I that wife that Jim sees by his side in the white world? If I say no, will I lose him forever? I love them both. How can love cause so much pain?"

"It is people who cause each other pain, I think," Linda said, thinking of Tad's bruised lip, and the baseball player, the one with cruelty in his eyes.

"Yes. If only my parents were like your grandparents were when your mother brought your father home."

Linda smiled. Perhaps that was where answers were, she thought. "We should ask our elders how it was at that time."

"A different time. With different people."

"But your father shook Jim Greene's hand. That feeling is in his heart, along with his anger. Promise me you will talk with my grandparents. Maybe the two worlds can be joined in your family too. And promise you will keep dancing with Guli and me, before you decide to become an old married woman?"

He friend hugged her with the same enthusiasm they'd had as children. "Of course, silly!"

They heard a faint knock at the door before Cousin Ella appeared.

"Get under those covers," she admonished her charges lightly. "There is good news. The road will open again by dawn, the men say."

"Did Ned phone his sister Shirley?" Rising Fawn asked.

"Yes. The storm is still there. She is afraid. But I called the *gadugi*. As soon as the storm subsides, the *gadugi* will send someone to check on her. And they will send a car for us before dawn. Let us get some sleep."

Linda remembered the old name that her cousin gave the Chero-kee free labor society. The *gadugi* was known as Community Club now, but its purpose was the same—to provide help to anyone in need. When Linda's family left Snowbird for north Georgia four years before, Cousin Ella told her that their family would be *gadugi* for any of the Snowbird people who traveled to their craft store. They treasured both the compliment and their responsibility.

Linda eased down into the covers beside her friend. From the room's other bed they soon heard their chaperone's light snore. Linda felt Rising Fawn's light touch at her shoulder.

"I knew you were not what some said after you left us, Ahyoka Ani-Waya," she whispered, honoring James Tassel's daughter Linda with her full Cherokee name, the one that included her mother's clan of the wolf. "I knew," Rising Fawn continued, "that you were not turning white."

Chapter Five

Tad woke from his doze, propped up between two tall men as Ned drove the old station wagon over twisting mountain roads. Predawn light began to filter through the dark forest around them. Every once and awhile Tad caught glimpses of swift-running creeks. There were few signs of human presence. Miles stretched between small cabins and simple houses of a newer construction. They were on the Snowbird Cherokee reservation now—small tracks of land scattered in and around public land and privately owned farms.

When they stopped for a breakfast break at an overlook, Tad stood on its ledge, staring at the Great Smoky Mountains.

The sun was rising over the sheltered cove. The old growth forest was a celebration of diversity, Tad realized as he raised his binoculars. He spotted yellow birch, sugar maple, beech, and Eastern hemlock trees. The deciduous trees had leafed out, their colors the gold greens of early summer. From their branches Tad heard the morning songs of thrushes and warblers through the blue haze.

Linda tapped his shoulder and handed him a cup of steaming coffee. "Here," she said as she added a generous slice of Irish raisin bread. "Guli almost snatched up the last of your mother's gift."

Tad left the binoculars hanging around his neck and took her offering, liberally spread with orange marmalade.

He smiled. "You remembered my weakness for this combination."

"I remember what keeps you from being a bear for half the morning."

Her quill earrings peeked out from her glistening hair. Three thin braids stood out, making it look even prettier than usual. She smelled great, as fresh as the dew of the morning.

Tad sipped the strong black coffee. "How could anyone be a bear this morning?" he said, turning back to the trees.

"Do you find it beautiful here, Tad?"

Tad placed his breakfast on an outgrowth of rock and pulled her to his side. She was troubled by something, he realized. "Of course."

"It is different than the beauty of Atlanta."

"Atlanta? Beautiful?"

"Of course. The lights, the movement. The tracks of roads and railways."

"You are full of surprises this morning."

"Yes? Is that bad?"

"No. I love surprises."

She laughed. "The mountain air sweetens you, Taddeusz Gist. Or maybe it is the marmalade."

Tad smiled at her exact pronunciation of his Polish name. He took another bite of his mother's bread. "What should I call you while I'm here, Linda?' he asked. "Should I switch to Ahyoka?"

He watched as she considered the question. Carefully, as she did everything. "Most of my relatives and friends use Ahyoka, especially at festival times. It is an honored name, and also belonged to Sequoyah's daughter."

"Did she also 'bring happiness?'"

Was she pleased that he remembered the translation of her Cherokee name?

"Oh yes. That woman helped her father Sequoyah as he developed our Cherokee language symbols. She learned them quickly too, then demonstrated their usefulness to her doubting elders."

"So, she was a bridge person too."

"Yes. I suppose she was. Between her people and their new written language."

Tad sat on the rock ledge to finish his breakfast. Linda sat cross-legged beside him. Her olive-green hiker shorts were complimented by her bronze toned legs.

"You'll be doing some translating for me this weekend, I hope," he said.

"*To hi u*. True."

"*Wa to*, Ahyoka," he thanked her.

"*O sta tsi ki*." She sounded impressed.

"*O sta*—?"

"*O sta tsi ki*. Good."

"All that for 'good?'"

Linda rolled her eyes. "Finish your breakfast, Buffalo Man."

As he did, she lifted the binoculars from around his neck and scanned the distance. "There are two reservations in the Eastern Nation," she explained. "We speak different dialects of our language. We Snowbird Cherokee speak Atali. On the Qualla Boundary they speak Kituhwa."

"Hey. That's your cousin Ella's last name."

"Yes."

"But she's Snowbird."

"Yes."

"How did that happen?"

She shrugged. "I have known people with the name Carpenter who never sawed a log, And Johnsons whose father's name was George or Peter. And that man who sings and writes silly songs, Roger Miller, I don't think he grinds grain."

Tad raised his hands, laughing. "All right, I see your point. Your cousin was not put on earth to make my life among the

Cherokee less confusing! So. I'll be hearing two versions of your language?"

"Three. Many of the Oklahoma Cherokee come to Harmony Festival, too."

"The Western nation."

"Exactly. Don't look so worried. Lots of our white Appalachian neighbors come too."

"And I can't understand them!" Tad sunk his head between his arms.

Linda laughed. "We all understand English, Tad."

He lifted his head. It was impossible to feel miserable when Linda was near. "Are we close to the festival grounds?"

"Yes." She pointed ahead with her chin. "That is Cad's Cove. If this mist dissolves a little more...there it is. See the steeple? The Church of the Dove's grounds is where the festival is held."

She returned Tad's binoculars. Tad spied a simple white clap-board church. It fit in well with the surrounding natural landscape, nestled in among ferns and thick tangles of rhododendron, flowing with white and purple blossoms.

"It was built by Methodists, back when the old wagon road went in about 1850," Linda explained. Now it is interdenominational. Pastor Tim McQuiston allowed us to dig a stomp ground on the property. It is a good place for Harmony Festival."

Tad liked Linda's practical, down-to-earth view of her own people's history. At the Mound Builders' dig site she'd talked about thousand-year-old skeletons as if they were her friends, separated only by chasms of time and culture.

Tad felt a tap at his shoulder. He turned to see his mitt, now pocketing a softball. He looked up into Guli's fierce dark eyes.

"Look. That is a real ball."

"As opposed to—?"

"Baseball." Guli spat out the word as if responsible for the wrongs perpetuated by white people against his since Columbus landed. "We have time for some catch, to get your glove used to making room for a real ball, if you would like."

Tad rose. Linda stayed silent, but her grin showed she approved of the progress he was making with securing the trust of her clan brother.

"All right, sure," he said, rising and promptly dropping the ball on his foot.

The view from their stop along the mountain road didn't reveal all the people Tad watched gathering as the station wagon moved slowly into the camp ground. Even more walked on both sides of the car as they approached the church. The storm had hit here too, he realized by the lines of wet clothing the women were hanging from

49

tree to tree, and in among the rhododendron bushes.

There was a small group near the ramp and steps of the clap-board church. They peered through their station wagon's windows. Among the faces, Tad spotted Linda's family. Her maternal grandparents Longknife stood smiling on either side of their elder daughter Theda's wheelchair. Behind a serene Theda stood Linda's parents. James and Naomi Tassel were holding hands and wore anxious looks.

Linda's Aunt Theda was the reason the family's home was in Georgia now. They'd left the Snowbird reservation land so that Theda could be near the Georgia hospital that specialized in multiple sclerosis therapy and research. The family started an extension of the nation's art and craft cooperative to earn a living and maintain their ties to home.

Linda's grandparents looked the same—wise, lively and interested in everything going on around them. Harry Longknife wore his characteristic red bandana wrapped around his chin-length iron grey hair. Tad wondered if Mr. Longknife brought some of his wonderful carved masks to the festival. Dolores waved her calloused beadworker's fingers in a shy wave. Linda's Aunt Theda looked a little more frail to Tad than she had last year when he'd visited the family's Georgia home and art gallery. But she smiled broadly. In her lap was a loaf wrapped in colorful blue and white gingham. Tad surmised it was her chestnut bread.

A group of colorfully-clad people now surrounded them and the station wagon, making a sound Tad didn't recognize.

"Turtle shell rattles, " Linda informed him at his ear. "They are happy that we came through the storm."

From the middle of the group, a man wearing a clerical collar, black sweater and jeans stepped forward. A blue and white beaded sash took the place of a belt.

"We offered prayers and burned tobacco toward your safe return," he told them.

Linda introduced the man as Reverend Tim McQuiston of the Church of the Dove. Reverent Tim was a tall, lanky guy with a full salt-and-pepper beard. Linda told Tad that his parents came from the Scots and Cherokee people. He had a lively step and dark, laughing eyes. Tad wondered if the church reflected a position of having a foot in both worlds as much as his dress and speech did.

Tad watched the pastor take Ned Socowah aside for a few private words. Their chaperone disappeared into the crowd.

"His sister must be worse," Guli speculated to Linda, close enough for Tad to hear. A glint came into his eyes. "I will take his place."

Guli for their chaperone? That was a fate worse than the brooding Ned. Ella Kituhwa giggled as if she'd heard Tad's thought before she and Guli formally led him to Linda's family.

When Linda's loving three-way embrace with her concerned parents ended, James Tassel shook Tad's hand.

"Welcome to Harmony Festival, Tad," he said.

"Thank you, sir."

James Tassel wore a blue denim work shirt with his sleeves rolled up. His hair was as blonde as Tad's own, but with streaks of silver at the temples.

Naomi Tassel squeezed Tad's arm. "I am so glad you are safe."

Tad smiled. Linda strongly resembled her mother. Her husband drew Naomi into a reassuring hug.

The Cherokee called all white people Anglos, whatever their country of origin, for the culture of the people who drove them away from their homeland and over their Trail of Tears. James Tassel was certainly Anglo, yet they accepted him as a member of their community. Tad wondered how many years that had taken. Could that acceptance ever happen for him?

Linda took his hand. "You will be fine here," she assured him quietly.

Tad greeted Linda's grandparents in nervous, Linda-coached Cherokee, which seemed to delight them. Then, he stooped beside Theda Longknife's wheelchair.

Tad held up a loaf of his mother's oatmeal bread that he'd salvaged from the wreck.

She smiled, offering the bundle in her lap. "Good trade," she pronounced with a slight wheeze in her voice as they made their exchange.

"It's good to see you again, Miss Longknife."

Tad felt the tips of Linda's fingers graze his back, then settle between his shoulder blades as he listened to her aunt.

"Rising Fawn and Guli and Ahyoka dance for me, for all of us who cannot," Theda said carefully forming the words.

"I'm looking forward to it."

"Come with us, get settled," Naomi Tassel invited.

Tad walked with the family along the wooden slated pathway. Men and women were adorning the church with strings of lights in blue, white, yellow and red. In the open field beside it, surrounded by pine wood groves, was the festival grounds. Tad looked at its open dance area, surrounded by squared off mounds. Each of the four mounds had steps leading up to sheds that sheltered benches within.

"Clan beds," Linda explained. "The festival grounds are set up like our traditional stomp ground, with a sacred square and fire, and the clan beds."

As they walked toward the camping grounds, Tad noticed people arriving, greeting friends, and setting up tents. Some came in trailers, some came in busses with the names of singing or dancing groups painted on their sides. The people already settled sat outside their tents or trailers, visiting with each other. Some were strumming guitars, banjos, mountain dulcimers and mandolins. Many played turtle or cow horn rattles, but Tad spotted a few tambourines and an Irish bodhran drum. Everyone was dressed casually. Tad felt an easy congeniality in the very air of the early morning.

The only hint of coolness came when Tad was introduced to Swimmer Reed, Rising Fawn's imposing, barrel-chested father. As his eyes scanned Tad, standing beside James Tassel, they squinted. His mouth became a taut, hard, line. Mr. Reed seemed to regard them as one, as if James was his, and not Linda's father, and he had distain for them both. Perhaps James was not as universally accepted as Tad had thought.

The man's tall, smiling wife, who Rising Fawn introduced as Peggy, was a study in contrast to her husband. She pressed Tad's hand in a warm welcome. "You are the boy who kept our Guli from being sent away from us to prison," she said.

"Not only me," Tad insisted, casting a sideways glance toward Guli. He didn't want the touchy subject of Linda's clan brother being held on suspicion of murder last year at the Mound Builders' dig site brought up. Their baseball versus softball rivalry was trial enough.

Tad had worked hard with Linda to discover Dr. Steffy's killer, with Linda being convinced of Guli's innocence from the beginning. Tad had taken longer to come around.

"The police would have realized their mistake eventually," Tad tried to deflect attention from himself.

"You have too much faith in your own people, maybe," Swimmer Reed said pointedly, turning Rising Fawn toward her family's tent.

Guli walked off to answer a camper's call to help peg down a tent pole.

"Shall we meet in an hour or so? At the north grove, for practice?" Linda called out to her dancing partners as they spun out of her orbit.

Guli grunted his agreement.

Rising Fawn looked up to her father, who nodded curtly, without stopping his pace.

Chapter Six

Linda watched the three little girls offer Tad their cow horn rattle. He inspected it carefully, then shook it close to his ear.

"Marbles?" he guessed at what was inside.

"No," Lydia Jumper answered, "too big!"

"Hmmm...bb pellets?"

All three shook their heads.

"Lizard lips? Panther hips? Alligator eyeballs?"

The three dissolved in laughter, bringing a crowd of little ones including Rising Fawn's three little sisters. "Dried corn! Dried corn!" they chimed out together.

Linda shook her head at his antics. Tad was going splendidly among her Harmony Festival friends and their families. How had she ever doubted that he would enjoy himself here?

Nearby an argument in Rising Fawn's family tent grew louder. Suddenly her friend burst from the tent's opening. Tad looked up from his gaggle of laughing children. Linda read anguish from her friend's expression. Her father followed.

"You, Linda Tassel!" he called out to her, using her father-given name. "Do not counsel my daughter in your White Indian ways." He glanced beyond her to where her younger daughters held on to Tad's sleeve.

"And look, this *A yo: wa ne: ka* of yours is like all the rest—he charms before he steals!"

Several men approached, both Cherokee and white, Guli among them.

"Think about your dishonor," Swimmer Reed commanded his daughter.

Rising Fawn looked into Linda's eyes as her own filled with tears. Then she ran off toward the woods. When Linda turned to follow, Swimmer Reed blocked her path.

"Let her think on this alone," he commanded quietly, sorrow mixing with the fire in his voice.

Every thought, every instinct told Linda to follow her friend.

Guli placed an arm around her shoulders. "Our practice time is close. Talk with her then. We will dance toward the return of harmony.

"Yes. Perhaps that would be best," Linda agreed. But was her clan brother right? Would obeying her heart only serve to widen the gap between Rising Fawn and her father?

She noticed Tad watching them. "I am sorry," she said.

He shrugged, confusion, not anger shining from his light eyes. Tad was a gift bringer, not a taker, not a stealer. Swimmer Reed was wrong about her Buffalo Man. She had trusted her life to Tad Gist. She would again, anytime. He was growing as dear to her as her own family. If her friend's father could not see him that way, it was because of his own sickness. She would have no part in it. But how could she help Rising Fawn?

She looked at Guli and Tad. "I need to visit my grandparents for a little while," she told them.

"Should we come?" Guli asked.

Linda smiled, looking from one to the other. "How am I so fortunate? *Hi gina lii.*"

"*Hi gina lii*? Tad repeated.

"Yes. Ha!" Linda nodded, turning. She heard Tad behind her.

"Wait a minute! What did you—what did I just say?"

"You said Ahyoka's words. You said you are our friend," Guli informed him.

"Oh? Oh, good."

Linda paused and looked over her shoulder. "Well friends, are you coming?"

Linda told Tad and Guli the story of Rising Fawn's romance with Jim Greene as they walked together over the festival grounds.

The sun was drying most of the morning dew. The craftspeople gathering already needed the protective shade of their tents. Linda led her friends to her grandparents' space. Dolores and Harry Longknife were sitting on aluminum lawn chairs, working diligently on their separate creations.

"We would like to hear a story Grandmother, Grandfather," Linda asked, standing formally beside the diminutive couple.

Dolores Longknife looked up from the beautifully curved basket she was making from honeysuckle vines. "What story, Granddaughter?"

"The one of my parents coming together."

Mrs. Longknife looked at her husband. Linda's grandfather was fitting a tuft of goat hair between the brows of his white oak carving of a Booger Mask. He nodded slowly. "*O sta tsi ki*," he said.

"It is good," Linda translated for Tad. "We can sit now."

The three took their place on the bloodroot mats at the feet of their elders, who went on with their work.

"James Tassel came for the ramps," Mr. Longknife began.

"No, old man, you forget," his wife chastised him. "James Tassel came over the mountain for a cure of the burn on his leg. The plantain leaves, then the ramps, then our daughter. That is the order of the story."

Linda's grandfather snorted. "It is still the ramps he loves best of the three."

Dolores Longknife closed her eyes, eyes set a little deeper than her mother's were. She began the remembering story.

"It was in winter he knocked on our cabin door. He was a college boy, from the North. He lived as a guest with a white family, part of a program of help and exchange. What was it called, granddaughter?"

"VISTA," Linda said, supplying the name of the idea of President Kennedy made real after his death—a domestic version of the Peace Corps: a year of service to help alleviate suffering and poverty.

"Yes. Not used to wood stoves, that's how the college boy burned his leg. It was not healing. They wanted to send him back home, but he loved these mountains, and all the people who lived here. So when the white medicine did not work, he came limping to our cabin like Sequoyah of old."

Her husband snorted. "I never heard you bring Sequoyah into the story before," he said.

Delores let out a girlish giggle. "Yes, it does get better with each telling, does it not, old man? We had a good supply of plantain stored up that winter," she continued. "We agreed to keep him one week."

"He never left," Harry Longknife said.

"Hi! You rush the story!" his wife objected.

"He ate us out of ramps. Tell that part."

Tad leaned closer to Linda. "What are ramps? And plantain?" he whispered.

"Ramps are a wild onion," Linda whispered back. Plantain leaves cured my father's burn."

Her grandmother's giggle sounded again. "Ramp soup, ramp salad. James liked whatever we did with them. But he also rose first in the morning to shovel the snow on the path to the out-house. And he played his banjo for the children all around. He knew how to pay proper court to our daughter," she defended her son-in-law.

"What did the people say of his courting, Grandmother?" Linda asked.

"Some said he would miss his life in the north. Others, that he was white and so would leave Naomi crying. We did not know many good white people, you see."

Harry Longknife's eyes lost their gruffness as he took up his part of the story. "But I trusted the white soldiers beside me on the battlefields of France. And I studied beside them in college after we came home. Yes, I was a college man, once! But I did not believe those teachers who said I was born of a savage people. And I returned home, to these mountains. James Tassel left his own people behind. We never knew an Anglo who sought us out. He confused us."

"He learned our stories and crafts and songs. And the language of the old ones," Dolores remembered. "With respect. The way we wished our own to carry on. He did not drink or smoke, or even swear. Our daughter gave him her heart. He could not help being Anglo. 'Should we cast him out because of something he cannot change?' we asked those who objected to the joining."

Her husband sighed. "We ask them that still. When we moved to Georgia some said, 'Ah, the White Indian will be greedy if we put him in charge of our people's craft store.'"

"They did not know him. Some still refuse to."

"Do you know Jim Greene?" Linda asked her elders quietly.

Her grandfather's pounding on his still faceless booger mask became louder. "Rising Fawn should respect her parents."

"Her parents are not of the same mind about Jim Greene," his wife stated. "And that was not Ahyoka's question."

Harry Longknife grunted. "Well, his motorcycle is not as loud as some," he conceded.

Tad turned to Linda. "A Yamaha ®? Black with red trimming? Reconditioned, mid-level displacement, on-the-road or off dual-purpose?"

Linda blinked. "Yamaha ®. Red. That's all I remember of how Rising Fawn described it."

"I think Jim Greene is here."

"At the festival?"

"Yeah. I mean I saw a nicely reconditioned bike parked behind that big maple tree outside the church grounds."

"Mr. Reed must have seen it too. That is what prompted the argument."

"Argument?" Delores Longknife asked.

"Between Rising Fawn and her parents, Grandmother. I worry about my friend."

"Jim Greene needs to develop a taste for ramps, maybe," her grandfather offered.

"What do you mean, Grandfather?"

"He wants to take Rising Fawn away. That is a hard thing for parents. The man comes into his woman's family. That is our way. Your father respected this. Developed a taste for ramps."

"But Jim Greene lost his factory job."

"Many lost jobs when the factory closed. He tries to show her people how much money he can make. That is part of life, but not the whole. We did not move to Georgia to make money, but to help Theda, and our community through the craft cooperative. That keeps your father a friend of the people. Jim Greene must prove himself a friend, before a provider."

"I will tell Rising Fawn what you have said. Thank you, Grandfather, Grandmother." Linda stood, took Tad's wrist to scan his watch. "It is past the time for our dancing rehearsal."

Guli made an unpleasant face. "Whites and their schedules! I suppose you cannot help being your father's daughter," he said. "This is Harmony Festival, Ahyoka. It does not run on clock time. Rising Fawn will be waiting for us."

Tad, who had been admiring his graduation gift, shoved his hands into his jeans pockets.

"You listen well, Buffalo Man," Dolores Longknife complimented him, even as his face was coloring. She took his sleeve as he tried to rise. "Go and practice your dancing, Guli, Ahyoka," she said. "Leave this one with us awhile. He looks hungry. I will make him a ramp salad."

Chapter Seven

Tad had eaten three bowls of Delores Longknife's ramp salad before the couple let him go to find Linda. The taste was growing on him, he had to admit. By the time he left their tent the numbers of people converging in the remote cove had mushroomed. Harmony Festival was not a craft fair, or a concert, or a religious event, but was somehow all three, and more. Tad watched people hug each other as if at a family reunion. Linda had said whole groups of Western Cherokee came— viewing this as a yearly visit to the ones who had escaped into the mountains of North Carolina during the Trail of Tears removals of the 1830s as just that—long lost family.

He liked how informally everyone dressed and how the children romped over the playground attached to the church with hardly a fight breaking out among them. Music wove through the air as he walked: percussion-driven stomps mixed with twangy bluegrass and harmonic gospel tunes. Laced through it came the scent of good outdoor cooking: tangy barbecue, boiled corn, Cherokee bean cakes, and the pungent smell of ramps.

Tad wandered into a tent where traditional Cherokee masks, jewelry, baskets, and pottery were on display. Their craftspeople sat behind tables, working on additional wares. Tad approached a jewelry display to find a gift for his little sister when a highly decorated peace pipe caught his attention.

The stone bowl was beautifully crafted, and reminded Tad of some of the pipe bowls he and Linda had unearthed at the Mound Builders' dig site last summer. Whoever the artist was knew a thousand-year-old tradition. Attached to the bowl was a wooden calumet adorned with partridge feathers, horsehair and shells. Suddenly the strong scent of gardenia was in the air.

"Beautiful, isn't it?" he heard a female voice drawl behind him. "But you're too late, darlin.' We have just settled on a price."

Tad turned to see a couple who looked as out of place as he would have at President Clinton's inaugural ball. The woman wore her hair in a high piled-on style that Dolly Parton might have thought a little too much. Her low-cut silk blouse was a riot of colors braced by a black leather vest punctuated by silver medallions. Her tight leather pants matched. She was having trouble maintaining her balance on the grassy surface of the craft tent's floor in her open-toed spike heel shoes.

"I was just admiring it," Tad said.

The man beside the overdressed woman was more casual in his purple Hawaiian shirt and white linen pants. He looked old enough to be the woman's father, but wide gold matching wedding rings announced them as husband and wife.

"What exactly do you admire, son?" the man asked in a matching drawl.

"How much the pipe honors tradition, going back to the pre-contact people."

The woman came forward. "There, you see honeybun, he's no threat, just a history student, no one we need worry about cutting into our little find!" Then she tapped her cheek with her well-manicured finger. "Oh my, that sounds rude doesn't it, darlin'? I mean no offense, Mr.—?"

"Tad. Tad Gist."

"Tad. So nice to make your acquaintance. We're the Tanners, Dora and Breman, up from Atlanta." She lowered her voice to a whisper. "Please excuse my husband. He sees one of us here and thinks we've got competition here at our little find."

"Us? Find?"

"Why, yes. You know. We stumbled onto Harmony Festival two years ago. What luck. Picked up a few trinkets to decorate our home. Well, we became the envy of our neighbors straight away. We decided to invest more each visit for my little bit of a shop on Peachtree."

"Indian stuff is hot right now," her husband informed Tad. "Since 'Dances With Wolves' came out."

"Fortunately," his wife continued, looking side to side, "most of them don't know that yet."

Breman Tanner frowned so deeply that his bushy brows formed a continuous line. "You are a student, Tad? Studying what? Archeology?"

Tad straightened his stance. "Yes, sir."

"Well then! What else can you tell us about our new piece of art?"

Tad didn't want to talk with this couple anymore. He wanted to find something pretty for Maggie, then find Linda. He hadn't even begun classes, never mind declared his major at Morris University. And he didn't like being taken into the Tanners' confidence just because he was white. But he didn't want them taking him for an ignorant kid either.

"The bowl is soapstone, which was used going all the way back to the people I study, the Mound Builders. The pipe looks like hickory, maybe dyed with bloodroot to get that color. The shells celebrate the trading network of the Eastern Woodlands Indians. That's how the shells got so far inland to these mountains—by trading routes."

"Well. You know a lot about the old time Indians, don't you, Tad?"

"No, sir. But I'm interested in them."

The woman tapped her lacquered finger at Tad's shoulder. "Why, the things you know could make our little finds a much richer experience to our cust—collectors."

"Why don't you ask the artists about the things you buy?" Tad suggested, wondering how long Linda and Rising Fawn and Guli would be practicing. He was growing awfully lonely for their company. Even Guli's.

"Why, the artists are not nearly as learned and congenial as you are Tad! Do you know that some of the older ones don't even speak English? Maybe you can fetch our itty-bitty tape recorder from the Winnebago, Breman dear?" she asked her husband sweetly. "I don't want to miss a word of what our Tad has to say."

Her husband grinned. "Sure. Say, let Dora buy you a Coke, son. Then you can take us on a tour of the items we've been considering for purchase. We'll pay you for your time, of course. Enough for you to buy something really nice for your girlfriend. You have a girlfriend, don't you, Tad?"

"Maybe both of you could visit our little shop, tell us about what we've got there. You'd like that, wouldn't you? Get yourselves out of these mountains? See Atlanta?"

"I live in Atlanta."

"You—?"

"Tad!"

It was Linda's voice, calling from outside the craft tent. "I've got to go," he told the Tanners, before rushing away from their company.

Linda had been running, Tad could tell from her flushed face and sweat-lined brow. He pulled her into the tent's shade. "Wow, that dancing is a workout, huh?" he asked as she caught her breath.

"Not dancing!"

"What do you mean?"

"We were not dancing. She didn't come to the meeting place!"

"Rising Fawn? You mean she gave up waiting and you missed each other?"

"No. She is gone from camp. Oh, Tad, come with me, please. I am afraid that something terrible has happened to my friend!"

Chapter Eight

Linda was grateful for Tad's trust as he took her hand in his. Guli met them as they entered the quiet grove past the north campground. Her clan brother looked worried.

"She did not forget our meeting," he said. "I talked with her mother. Rising Fawn left her family tent with her leggings and rattles."

"Leggings?" Tad asked them.

"We wear goat hair leggings," Linda told him. "For sure-footedness. And turtle shell rattles strapped to them. If she took those things, she was coming here."

Guli grunted. "Let's spread out and look around our practice place for signs of her."

Tad and Guli left the western section of the grove to her. Linda tried to breathe easier, walking through its stillness, watching the ground for signs of Rising Fawn. She scanned pine needles lightly trod upon by festival goers passing through.

As she entered a more forested section, Linda saw that a few yellow trilliums were still blooming among the phacelia in the grove's shade. She caught the trilliums sweet lemony scent growing stronger. The flowers' mottled leaves were broken off and on the ground, along with several of the three-petal flowers. And the pine-needle-strewn floor of the forest was more disturbed.

Linda went to her knees. "Tad! Guli!" she called.

She heard their footfalls coming from opposite directions. She continued to scan the ground. They reached her side at almost the same time.

"What do you think?" she asked. "A struggle?"

Guli crouched beside her. "Maybe. But maybe a deer resting. Or children playing." He cleared away some of the disturbed area until he reached soil. Something lighter than the rich loam emerged. Linda hesitated. Guli pulled it forth. It was Rising Fawn's legging.

His breath caught before he spoke. "Maybe she was dancing. Maybe it flew off into these bushes and she could not find it."

His words did not relieve the tight feeling in Linda's chest. It was compounded when they looked up to see Tad lifting the shining silver necklace from the branch of a white rhododendron bush.

Guli stood, inspected it. "That's a *Ani: yo: wa ne: ka* thing," he pronounced disdainfully. "Good silver. But store-bought, machine made. Not likely to belong to—"

"It is Rising Fawn's," Linda said.

Guli folded his arms. "I never saw her wearing it."

"She wore it under her clothes, because it is a gift from Jim Greene. And look, the clasp is broken."

Tad swirled the necklace into the open palm of Linda's out-stretched hand.

"Something bad has happened here, I think," she said.

Swimmer Reed hunched over the card table, staring down at his note pad. But Linda didn't think he saw them.

"I must speak for the anti-gambling faction at today's debate," he said. "It is a sacred trust. I must be ready with our arguments. Rising Fawn has gone off for a little while, that's all. She has done it before. Often when I'm charged to speak for the people. She does not think of us, only of getting a job at a casino, maybe. That's what this boy has done."

"I don't think she is with Jim Reed, sir," Linda said.

"His motorcycle is gone. You asked. No one has seen it since this morning. You told me this yourself."

"Yes, but—" How could she make him understand, Linda wondered. She took a deep breath. Tad gave her a smile that urged her to keep trying. She opened her hand. "Jim Greene gave her this necklace,

73

Mr. Reed. Rising Fawn would not have left without it."

Swimmer Reed frowned. "She lost it, that's all. She is not careful or considerate with gifts. Even his."

"But she promised, sir," Guli tried. "She promised to dance the Butterfly Dance with us."

Mr. Reed's eyes did not leave her. "You have been away from us, Linda Tassel. Her promises mean nothing anymore. You no longer know her."

It is your anger that comes between you and knowing your own daughter, Linda wanted to tell him. But she lowered her gaze before her elder's scrutiny. "It is true that I have been living away from Snowbird for a long time," she said, with more calmness than she felt. "But Rising Fawn and I have been friends since we were babies. She hugged me when she promised to stay for the festival, to dance with us. I felt the strength of that promise in her bones."

Swimmer Reed stood slowly. He stared at the wall of the canvas tent, rubbing a circle at his temple with his calloused thumb. "All right. Tell the police in Roaring Rock what you have found. But tell them what everyone else is talking about—that Jim Greene was here, and is now also missing. See what the police make of that."

"Won't you come with us, sir?" Guli asked.

"I will stay, prepare to speak for the people. Against more Anglo corruption. This is what comes when we leave the land." He made a gesture of despair with his big, farmer's hands. "We get soft and loose our balance. We form alliances with corrupt strangers."

Linda knew that Swimmer Reed was lashing out at her because of his grief, but she still felt a sting. But she also felt comfort from the presence of Tad and her clan brother beside her as they walked out of the tent.

Peggy Reed met them there. Her eyes were anxious. Her youngest child, Amity was tucked into her baby sling. "May I go with you to Roaring Rock?" she asked quietly.

Linda smiled. "Having you with us will be a great help."

"I put Esther in charge of the others. Seth will bring the car seat for Iris. We are ready."

Peggy Reed did not turn back to talk to her husband about her decision. Linda didn't remember Swimmer Reed being so unyielding to his large family. How had it started? She wondered if Rising Fawn also stepped out with Jim Greene in this way of her mother—by not asking for permission she was sure not to get.

The iron-handed way Mr. Reed ruled his family was not typical of the Cherokee, Linda thought. It was more like some of the male dominant white families she had observed, the ones Swimmer Reed claimed to hate.

"We should tell Ned and Ella about Rising Fawn and what we are doing," Guli said.

Linda nodded. Yes, it would be bad manners not to keep their chaperones informed.

They reached the craft tent where Cousin Ella, her arm in a sling, was looking over the clay pots of her apprentices. The sweet-faced woman nodded her approval, then told them, "You need not look for Ned. He was called back home to tend to his sister and her grieving sickness. The *gadugi* will meet on it. With Shirley, this gambling business, and now Rising Fawn. we will need plenty of good medicine this year, I think," she said with a weariness in her voice.

Then Ella smiled. It was like one of her grandmother's smiles and lit up her whole face. "We need not have any concern for you young ones, go. Do what needs doing." She waved them off with her good hand.

Linda was grateful for her elder's blessing. Tad was too. He smiled wide. "Thank you, ma'am," he told her.

"How long has your daughter been missing, Mrs. Reed?" Sheriff Harrison asked.

"Since this morning."

"But it's barely afternoon."

Three-month-old Amity began to fuss in her mother's arms. Peggy Reed turned away to pull the cotton blouse out of her colorful skirt's waistband in order to nurse the baby discretely. As she did, Linda tried to explain the circumstances again to the large, starch-smelling man. "We thought we should come here when we saw the signs in the woods, and Rising Fawn's necklace. Do you want to come and look, sir?"

"She wore this silver necklace safely tucked under her clothing, you said?"

"Yes."

"The clasp is broken. If you were late for this dance rehearsal, and she was waiting. Might she have started dancing herself? That would have disturbed the pine needles, right?"

"Well, yes," Linda admitted.

Amity was content now. Sheriff Harrison directed his remarks to Peggy Reed again. "Now, Ma'am, picture this with me now. Say the necklace broke, fell off. Your daughter might not realize it was missing, especially if she was looking for the legging she'd kicked into the bushes."

He ran his finger over the necklace's twinning strands of silver, just as Linda herself had done when they'd first discovered it. But the conclusion he was coming to was so different from the threatening feeling she had gotten. Linda's hope was fading fast.

"It's a pretty thing," the sheriff said affably. But light."

"She treasured it, sir. She would know if it was gone."

Tad and Guli touched each of her shoulders from their places on either side of her. Harrison looked up at them, his eyes narrowing. He felt threatened. By her. By her men's support and comfort.

He returned to regarding the notes he'd been taking. "Now, this Jim Greene. I seem to remember him as one of the Aurora factory troublemakers. Complaining about safety after one of your people got himself killed there."

"I do not know about that, sir," Linda admitted.

"You've been off the reservation for awhile, little lady. That factory employed Cherokee and white, working side by side. It meant a lot to this community. Now there's a lot of people who lost their jobs to some Mexicans or Chinese when the place shut down." He turned to Peggy Reed. "How's your recollection, Ma'am?"

"The safety walkout lasted one day," she replied quietly. "And it was not against the law."

"Didn't say it was. Jim Greene was our accident victim's floor supervisor. Real law-abiding fellow, right down to that nice quiet motorcycle of his. Not even a noise annoyance call from his neighbors. But if he's taken off with your little girl, Ma'am, we can talk. We can authorize the state police."

"Rising Fawn is not a minor."

"She's not?"

"No. She is our oldest child. She turned eighteen in April."

The big man frowned. "Then what are we talking about?"

"She is gone."

"For a few hours? A person over the age of eighteen is not considered missing unless it's been over twenty-four hours."

"We think something bad has happened to her," Linda tried. Stupid, she told herself. This is the kind of talk white people laugh at—Indian gut feelings, without sufficient evidence. To Sheriff Harrison, she was surely an uppity Cherokee, standing between her clan brother and her white boyfriend, telling him his business.

He turned to Mrs. Reed and spoke softly. "You know, Ma'am, I think these young folks upset you with their overactive imaginations."

He frowned before shifting his gaze back to Linda. "You haven't convinced me that I need to come out there to the festival grounds."

"But what if she's been kidnapped?"

"No ransom note?"

"No, sir."

"And the only disturbance has been due to her argument with her father over this boyfriend?"

"Well, yes, but—"

"Listen young lady, That festival has swelled the population of Roaring Rock three times over. And with this string of fires of suspicious origins reported lately."

"Fires?"

"Yes. Maybe you're not in such close contact with your tribe to hear about them? Almost cancelled the festival. A general store and three homes—two white and one Cherokee cabin. That's the only blessing— looks like we won't have a race war as our arsonist doesn't appear to discriminate. We'd sure like to put an end to this before the summer heat lends a hand and this pretty little piece of North Carolina gets burned off the map.

"Listen. I sympathize. I'm a daddy myself. But we're a police department of two and a half officers. We're too pressed right now to be dusting for fingerprints in pine needles to find a little girl who has likely just taken a joyride off the reservation with her boyfriend."

He closed his notebook.

Linda was helping Mrs. Reed strap her baby into the car seat when Tad turned around from the front passenger side.

"Do you think Amity can hold out with us a little while longer?" he asked her mother.

"She is content. Why?"

"Guli and I have been talking. He knows Jim's place is on Fontana Lake. How far is that from here Guli?"

"Four, maybe five miles," he answered. "And I know which trailer is his."

"Why don't we do what we were hoping the police would? Investigate possibilities."

They all nodded their agreement, and even little Amity sighed in her sleep.

Jim Greene's trailer was old—one of those silver ones that looked like 1950s diners. There was no sign of a motorcycle. The grounds were well kept and its spot on the lake was a choice one. Beside the trailer sat a small wooden shed.

"That's his shop. Jim Greene does repairs," Guli explained as he pulled the car up to the trailer.

They all got out as Mrs. Reed slipped little Amity into her baby sling.

Linda climbed two cinder block steps to knock at the door. There was no answer. Linda looked through the lace-curtained window beside the door. She saw a simple, well kept living area and kitchen. On a small table beside the couch sat two in the Jean Hager book series, set in the Oklahoma Cherokee nation. Linda smiled. Jim was showing more than an interest in mystery novels. Propped next to the books was a framed photograph of Rising Fawn in her Butterfly Dance regalia, her fancy shawl flying, her face lit with delight.

"He's gone away," Linda heard behind her. She stepped back from the window, embarrassed by her own rude behavior.

A woman of middle years with smiling eyes, dressed in blue and white polka dots approached. "You folks friends of Jim's?" she asked.

"Yes," Peggy Reed said quickly, introducing them all to Helen Gilmartin, a neighbor from beyond a small stand of pine trees to the west of Jim Greene's property.

"What a pretty baby! Name?"

"Amity."

"And are you and Amity relatives of that sweet girlfriend of Jim's?"

"Mother and sister."

"Well, Jim will be sorry he missed you all. I've just been watering Rising Fawn's garden out back."

"Rising Fawn's garden?"

"Do you think that motorcycle maniac would think of a garden on his own? Not unless it grows spark plugs! I always told him I thought the place needed a little color, but he thought I meant custom trim, I think!

Now he asks me to water it when he's away. Your daughter is expanding his horizons, Peggy."

"Did he say how long he'd be gone this time, Ma'am?" Tad asked quietly.

"Just that he'd be overnight in Marysville. He had a job interview."

"Did he say where? What company?"

"He might have but…sorry, I don't remember. Hate the thought of losing him to Marysville, maybe I didn't listen hard enough if he told me." Her smile faded. "Is there something wrong?"

"My daughter is missing," Peggy said simply.

"Oh. Oh, dear, I'm so sorry. You don't think…? Mrs. Reed, I've been neighbors with Jim Greene for two years now. He's a good boy. Not so much as a wild party. And he's fixed my lawn mower twice and never taken a cent from me, only in return favors, like watering Rising Fawn's garden. I think you should look somewhere else for your daughter."

Something had changed in the woman's tone. She was standing guard now, Linda thought. They weren't going to get in that trailer or shed.

Tad must have sensed it too. "Thank you for your help, Ma'am," he said. "We'll let you get back to your watering."

Chapter Nine

"I need to bathe in the creek and release the poison of that place," Guli said, as they approached the main performance tent of the festival.

Linda nodded. Tad watched Guli stomp off. "What does he mean?" he asked. "What poison place?"

"The police station."

It was not a great idea, going to the police, Tad realized now. Did Linda blame him for it?

She nodded toward the big tent. "I must tell them, inside."

"Tell them what?"

"Guli is scheduled next. A hoop dance demonstration."

"All those people are waiting for him to dance?"

"Yes."

"And he's gone swimming?"

"He needs to, Tad."

"Won't they be angry?"

"Not the ones who stay and wait. The ones who leave? They do not belong here."

Did she include him in that number? "I'm sorry for what happened at the police station."

She touched his shoulder. "I know. But I am worried about my friend."

"I am too."

"Are you? You do not think Sheriff Harrison is right?"

"Of course not. What does he know of your friend? I trust your instincts over what he thinks about Rising Fawn, or any Cherokee woman."

"You will help me find her?"

Over her shoulder he saw Breman Tanner approaching, with Dora close behind. Way to ruin a moment. He barely had time to take Linda's hand. "What am I, some tourist?" he demanded with a smile as he sighed in the direction of the couple.

They hadn't been spotted yet. She pulled Tad toward the dance tent.

Most of the audience sitting under the bright yellow and white awning were admiring playful babies or teasing small children who ran around them. But Linda drew the attention of all as she mounted the wooden stage's steps and quietly explained that Guli's dance was delayed.

A few white people left the tent, complaining about "Indian time." But those remaining nodded, opened drinks, called over children and began opening picnic baskets. Tad found himself surrounded by some of the turtle rattle children he'd met that morning. He wished he'd brought the beanbags that he and his sister Maggie practiced with together. He borrowed three scarfs from little girls' finery and demonstrated a few passes. Soon more scarves appeared and he had a dozen eager juggling students.

Linda shook her head, laughing, before she walked over to the display tables of dancers' regalia. He watched her glide her graceful fingers over the maple leaf beadwork designs on her friend's Fancy Dance shawl.

The new jugglers were returning the favor—showing Tad a cat's cradle-like string game when he saw the Tanners enter the tent and head straight for Linda. The deer pattern he had almost achieved collapsed into a jumble of twine before he excused himself from the children's company.

Tad saw Linda stiffen as he caught the end of Breman Tanner's question. "So, if the girl's disgraced, might her father be open to selling her costume?"

Tad wanted to punch the guy's lights out. "We're sure her family's not thinking about that right now, Mr. Tanner," he said between his teeth, before he felt Dora Tanner's fingernails clawing his shoulder.

"Won't you introduce us to your friend, Tad?"

The couple were guests of the festival. It was not his place to make them feel unwelcome, he reminded himself as he introduced Linda.

"Why, you must be part of the Tassel family who run the Phoenix Craft Shop over in Cartersville," Dora Tanner said.

"I am Naomi and James Tassel's daughter."

Dora sounded too delighted. Did she see the shop as a rival of the couple's business?

"It is more of a tribal co-operative," Linda continued pleasantly.

"We've been hearing so much about you! Your delightful father said you would be dancing. And he gave us a brochure and directions to your shop! Oh we must visit!"

"You will be welcome," Linda told her. She was distracted now, as she spotted Guli standing by one of the tent's poles. He was in full regalia, with his hoops slung over his shoulder. "If you will excuse me," she said politely, " I need to help my clan brother begin his program."

Tad thought he saw a private apology from her eyes as she left. He didn't mind being left with the obnoxious Atlantans, as long as she knew he was not one of them.

Guli stood at solemn attention on the small platform stage as Linda introduced him. He wore an intense blue vest and fringed breechcloth. Both were decorated with red, yellow, blue, and white designs in a series of triangles. His thirty-six hoops were marked with bands of colors at their four direction points. His white moccasins were beaded almost solid with the same triangle designs. Tied above them were a pair of goatskin leggings like the one they'd discovered in the bushes as they searched for Rising Fawn. Instead of turtle shell rattles above them, Guli wore a line of six small cow bells strapped just below his knee. There were also plain black straps around his wrists and his powerful upper biceps. His sleek, freshly washed hair was out of its usual ponytail and flowed freely past his shoulders.

Guli looked magnificent. As Linda explained, first in Cherokee, then in English, the coming metamorphosis that Guli would achieve with his hoops, Tad once again was thankful that kinship ties kept Guli and Linda from thinking romantically of each other. Would he have a chance, were it not for the clan-based taboos?

Tad watched, along with the attentive audience, as Guli went through his series of changes in slow motion.

Linda directed her attention to the children sitting on blankets in front of the first row seats. "What is my brother now?" she asked them.

"*Utsonati!*" several cried out.

"*Ha yu!*" Linda confirmed. "The rattlesnake!"

Guli manipulated his hoops, and added more. "And now?" Linda asked their audience.

"*Gyna*," one boy called out. "*Gugue?*" another tried.

"It is not owl, or quail," Linda translated.

Guli frowned, then put a hoop in his teeth and jerked his head in a pecking motion.

A small girl proclaimed, "*Tallalla!*"

Linda gifted the girl with one of her radiant smiles. "Exactly, a woodpecker!"

Dancing staccato, using every muscle it seemed, Guli made a deer, wolf, flowers, and even sunshine with his dazzling hoops. The children clapped for his skill and for their own ability to recognize the subjects of his movements. None of the hoops tangled in his fringe, hoops, bells, or gleaming hair. The flying goat hair leggings did indeed seem to keep him sure-footed. Tad was astonished when he used all thirty-six hoops to create his final metamorphosis— turning himself into a globe of the earth itself.

When he was finished, Linda called all the children who had participated in naming the forms up on the stage. All received the audience's enthusiastic applause.

"Why don't they get out of the way, so I can get a picture of the dancer?" Breman Tenner groused.

"That would be rude, to stand alone, sir," Tad found himself explaining. "The Cherokee don't value individual achievement in the same way we do. They're all about striving for the benefit of the group."

"Hmmm, sounds communist to me," Mr. Tanner muttered.

His wife made a tsk sound. "Why, it's no wonder the poor things can't work their way out of those dingy little cabins, being forced to think that way."

Tad head his own teeth grinding.

He felt Mr. Tanner's hand on his shoulder. "We are so fortunate to have you as our scout, Tad. And we'll make it worth your while, I promise."

Tad turned. "I don't understand."

"Oh no," his wife assured him. "It's we who don't understand. Things like, could you tell us what will become of that wonderful shawl of the girl who disgraced her family by running off?"

"Running off? Who told you that?"

"Why, it's the buzz all over, darlin'! They are such a happy people, at least at festival times. So the argument that little one had—"

"Her name is Rising Fawn."

"Yes, of course. The argument Rising Fawn had with her daddy stuck out amid all the tranquility. And the boyfriend was here, and now they're both gone, so what's everyone to think?"

"I'm not concerned with everyone, Ma'am. I only know that Linda is worried about her friend."

"There, you see? You're no communist, caring about what everyone thinks! Neither is your girlfriend, only concerned about her friend. That's her father coming out in her, I should think. Such a shame she didn't get his looks, too."

"Now, Dora," her husband said sternly, nodding toward Tad. "Beauty's in the eye of the beholder.

"Oh, I do forget myself! I meant, of course, for that sweet girl's own sake in getting along in this cold cruel world."

Tad felt caught in the vise of their talk. Then his arm felt the actual vise of Guli's grip. "*Hi hwi lo hi U hoh saa!*" Linda's kinsman muttered gruffly.

The Atlanta couple backed away from them. "What does he want, Tad?" Breman asked nervously as his wife clung to him.

Tad grinned. "I'm being invited to a Cementation ritual."

"What in heaven's name is a—"

But he didn't have time to respond as Guli almost carried him bodily from the tent.

91

When they got out of the Tanners' sight, Guli released his hold.

"What do you know of the Cementation ritual?" he demanded.

Tad shrugged. "I needed one of the rituals that sounded gruesome. Am I glad you showed up. Those two give me the willies!"

Guli smiled grimly. "So. Ahyoka was right. You needed rescuing. Done. Now we're even."

"Even? For helping you beat a murder rap last year?"

"Sure. If those people are demons to you."

"Well. I guess you have a point."

"Ahyoka said to meet her at the pine grove. And bring lunch."

After visiting several of the food stations, they bought enough hot corn, barbecue, and birch beer to satisfy Linda's good appetite besides their own.

"Your dance was great," Tad told her quiet clan brother.

More silence. Well, at least he didn't criticize the way he expressed the compliment. But his eyes kept scrutinizing the trail. Finally, he lifted his head.

"You did not understand what I really said back there, did you?"

"Nope."

"I told you to get out of there. And be strong."

"Yeah?"

Wow, the gruff tone had sounded a lot more threatening to Tad's ears than that.

"You and I?" Guli said quietly. "We are not yet ready for the Cementation ritual, I think."

Tad felt like an idiot. Of course. The Cementation ritual involved two men exchanging garments and valued items to "cement" their everlasting friendship. It even symbolized the good relations between the Above Beings and the people.

"Guli. I was just so happy to see you and I wanted us as far away from the Tanners as we could get without them following. I didn't mean to say I thought we were ready."

His companion grunted and narrowed his focus further. "Maybe, someday," he said.

"Sure, maybe. I mean, It would honor me," Tad tried to say it in Cherokee polite.

When they reached the grove, Linda seemed to sense a difference in them, because she hugged them both. And it wasn't just because the barbecue smelled so good.

Chapter Ten

"Let us go over what we've got," Linda suggested, as she tried to talk about her friend's disappearance in this place that was haunted with what happened to Rising Fawn.

Tad began. "We had scattered pine needles, but now the ground is pretty trampled over."

"While we went to town to get no help from the police," Guli finished, with a growl toward Tad.

Linda touched his arm. "We all agreed to go. We thought it would help."

"We were wrong."

"We have alerted Sheriff Harrison, at least. And we can return, if we find something more compelling."

"After twenty-four hours." There was belligerence in Guli's tone. But Linda felt a calm stillness radiating from Tad.

"Yes," she agreed. "What else?"

"We've got the legging and the necklace."

She lifted both from her bag and put them into Tad's hands. "How did Rising

Fawn loose these? Do you think she was dancing, while she waited for us?"

"Yes, with the Anglo Jim Greene."

The three of them turned to see who had said the words. A little bright-eyed girl seemed rooted in the shade of a honeysuckle bush. Was she one of the children Tad had charmed with his juggling scarves?

"Lydia? Lydia Jumper?" Linda called her softly.

She did not move.

"You are very still. Like a good tracker," Linda tried.

"I liked the dance. I did not mean to be bad. And I left when they started kissing."

"You were not bad," Linda said. "But we need to know everything you remember. Please sit beside us."

The little girl eyed Tad and Guli. "We are Rising Fawn's friends, Lydia," Linda tried. "What disturbs you about talking with us?"

"Rising Fawn teaches us—Creek Mayes and Katie Glory and me—how to strap on the turtle shells. She shows us how to make our legs strong, so they will hold more rattles without slipping. Has she gone away like you did, Ahyoka? To live among the Anglos?"

Linda felt a dullness creeping around her heart. Guli frowned, but his voice was soft as he squatted beside Lydia Jumper. "Who says that?" he asked the girl.

"Rising Fawn's daddy. He yells it, from inside their tent."

Guli's voice softened further. "Ahyoka has not gone away from us. She helps her parents care for her Aunt Theda, near the doctors who might know how to keep her among us. And she sells our pots and jewelry and baskets so that we have the swings and slide beside Harmony church. We see them at our festival times and at New Moon trading days. They trade with us fairly instead of that thief Wikerson, who we ran off, remember?"

"Yes. Soon my quill earrings will be good enough to trade, Mr. Tassel says!"

"There, then. Ahyoka is not from us, is she? She even brings another decent Light Eyes to our festival. This one, when the police held me, he told them I was not bad, and use my knives to dance, not to hurt. He and Ahyoka found the one who did the hurting, and the police let me go."

The girl finally ventured out from her hiding place. "I have heard that story," she said. "But not from you."

"This is the first time I have told it."

"You should tell it bigger. Four Bears tells it much bigger—with skeletons and bullets and lots of blood."

Guli glanced back at Linda as she was trying to stifle her giggle. He sighed and returned his attention to the girl. "That does not interest me. I told it to hear your story. Let's trade, Lydia Jumper."

The little girl took Guli's hand. He led her to Tad and Linda. Linda wondered if her clan brother could sense the joyful thanks she felt. He brought Lydia between Tad and herself, then sat across from the little girl. He leaned his arms on his knees so that their eyes were level. It was an honor that Linda suspected was not lost on the eight-year-old.

"It was this morning. I was walking through the grove," she began. "I heard the turtle rattles first and I thought the sound came from our teacher, Rising Fawn. No one else can make so many rattles sound so clearly. I wanted to watch her, because she was lost in the dance. When she teaches us, she is not so free. She goes slowly, so we can follow her. And she does not leap so high. I wanted to see those leaps, so I watched from my hidden place. Jim Greene came. He almost touched my sleeve as he passed me."

Linda tried to picture the scene in her mind. "Where were you?"

"The same place you found me."

"And Rising Fawn was here, in this clearing?"

"Yes."

"Jim Greene did not notice you?"

"No. He was looking at Rising Fawn. Like the hunter follows the deer. He is a hunter, Rising Fawn told us, who left venison on the doorstep of Shirley Cutcheon after her man died."

"Did he speak? Did he ask Rising Fawn to go away with him?" Guli asked the girl.

"Yes, I think so. He could not wait any more, he said. He had to go to Tennessee, for a job there. Rising Fawn shook her head, and cried."

"Cried?" Linda whispered, fear clutching her heart.

"He said sad things, not mean ones, I think, Ahyoka. Sad and quiet and rumbling, like the sounds from his motorcycle. When Rising Fawn cried, he tried to tease her."

"How?"

"I don't know, I did not understand it. It was mostly whispering words, and tickling at her side. That's when she untied her legging, the right one, I think, and tied it to his leg, and they danced together."

"Her shawl dance?" Guli asked.

"No. A white person dance, with the rattles for the beat. You know, rock and roll."

Guli grunted. Tad's smile matched Linda's own.

"When the dance finished, the kissing started. That's when I left. They were lost in each other. I knew they would not see me. That's all," she finished her story.

"Did you see this necklace?" Linda asked, showing the little girl Rising Fawn's treasure.

"Oh, yes. Rising Fawn pulled it out of her blouse as soon as she saw him."

"And it stayed around her neck? It did not fall off when they danced?"

"Oh, no. It sparkles. I saw it on her the whole time."

"Thank you for telling us what you saw," Guli said.

"That's not why I came here. I was waiting to give you the message, Guli."

"A message, For me?"

"Yes. Pastor Tim says he thinks you should come. And take notes."

"Notes? On what?"

"The meeting at the church. About the gambling. The gambling talk around camp is not good for harmony, Pastor Tim says. He wants everybody to speak, but not around separate campfires. In church, all together, instead, remember?"

Guli smiled. "Ah, yes. It's good I have my little wife to remind me," he teased.

The girl hid her face behind her hands and giggled. When she came out, she looked stern. "Come. The festival chief says you write clear and fast. She wants you to write the talk out."

Linda took her clan brother's arm. "Is this some new talent of yours, Guli?"

He sniffed indignantly. "This little one's grandmother is the scribe, but she can't read her own handwriting, maybe. And with my ears and hand busy, she keeps me out of the thick of the arguments, maybe. Will you come?"

Linda looked to Tad, who nodded. "Sure. Go on ahead, Guli, we're almost finished here."

Chapter Eleven

Tad followed Linda's footsteps as she circled the last place Rising Fawn had been seen. She clutched her friend's necklace and legging as they walked. The rattles made a lonesome sound.

"Dried corn?" Tad asked.

Linda lifted her head. "Corn?"

"In the turtle rattles?"

"Oh, no. Rising Fawn and I, we use river gravel. Some use marbles, or sandstone. But we like the sharp, clean sound of the.." her voice faltered, "the river gravel."

"We'll find her, Ahyoka," he tried to comfort her.

"Even after what Lydia saw, you still don't think she has run off with Jim Greene?"

"No. It sounds to me like they met here, her asked her to go, but she decided to stay. They danced after, so it doesn't sound like he left with hard feelings about it."

"But we don't know what happened, after."

"No. Maybe I'm just relying on the good sense of you butterfly dancers. And your taste in Anglo men."

Linda turned away, smiling. "You do not talk like an Anglo here, Buffalo Man. So many polite 'maybes.'"

"Yeah. my debate teacher picked up on that. 'Gist! Too many qualifiers! Weakens speech!' Polite in Cherokee translates to compromising and trying to achieve consensus. Deadly sins in debate division of Speech Club."

"Poor Tad. What did you do?"

"Gave them what they wanted. I still think as I please, but I need that Speech Club pin to help me get into Morris University."

"It is a good thing I did not need that pin."

"Hey, are you lording your better grades over me?"

"No, no! That's not what I meant."

"I know. Linda, I'm teasing you."

"Oh. Oh, good. I am so glad we are planning to go to the same school, Tad."

"Me too."

"We will see much more of each other. And we can talk with each other as we please."

"Yeah. The letters and phone calls and visits have been great. But I'd like to see how we do day to day."

Tad loved the small musical sounds her glass beaded earrings made as she continued to scan the ground.

She finished her circle. "What does finding these things, in this place, mean? This necklace had a measureless value to Rising Fawn, Tad. She would not have left it hanging on a branch."

"Unless she wanted you to find it," Tad suggested.

"Why is the clasp broken?"

"Lydia told us it was on her when she danced with Jim. I don't think it broke during butterfly dancing or rock and roll. I think it happened after."

Linda's eyes blinked twice. "When someone else was here. The one who took her."

"Yes."

"She left two pieces of herself. Her Cherokee self and her love for Jim Greene. To tell us to find her. She is counting on us, Tad."

"We won't let her down," Tad said quietly, offering his hand.

She took it. "Let's go to the meeting. We have to discover who did this."

The inside of the Church of the Dove reminded Tad of a Quaker meeting house he and his mother had visited when she was doing a report on the Earth Care Witness environmental activism of the local

Society of Friends. Here, although built in the traditional Protestant everybody-faces-the-altar, the seating was adjusted to wooden benches all facing the middle. There was no altar, or even a lectern, only floorspace. The walls were whitewashed and the eight windows were of plain glass. A single wood burning stove in one corner was ready kept to provide some heat in the place come winter.

The tall windows were so clean that the trees and meadows beyond sparkled. The single stained-glass window at the end of the church depicted a pearly white dove in full flight, an olive branch in its beak.

The church benches were full.

"There are some outside mediators here," Linda explained. "But they recognize that this will be about internal Snowbird concerns."

The crowd quieted around them. Yes, Tad noticed only a few white people. But Dora and Breman Tanner stood out. What were they doing here?

Although the physical set up made it hard to see who the leaders were, Tad noticed Guli sitting next to a guy looking over some papers while bouncing a baby on his knee. Next to him, a woman of about sixty held the baby's chubby little fist while regarding the whole crown with a serene, motherly air. Beside her, Pastor Tim was counting heads.

Guli had a yellow legal-sized pad in his lap and was whittling his pencil's point with his pocket knife. When he saw Tad and Linda, he nodded toward the bench where her family sat. They looked up and shifted until there was room for them both. Linda's Aunt Theda sat close by the bench, in her wheelchair by the church's doors. "Any progress in finding Rising Fawn?" she whispered after they'd greeted her.

"No, Aunt Theda," Linda told her.

"Guli tells us the police won't help unless there's a blood trail."

Linda winced.

"He's right," Tad said.

"And her father won't even let her name be spoken, the old fool!"

Tad must have shown his surprise, for Theda Longknife patted his hand. "A privilege of age and the infirm, Tad—to be blunt. Do not listen to any of them. Follow where Rising Fawn leads. Keep looking."

Tad watched Guli lean over and speak to the man with the baby and the papers, who in turned whispered in the ear of an older woman. She stood and the room immediately quieted.

Linda leaned into Tad's shoulder. "She is Nina Jumper, little Lydia's grandmother. She is Festival chief. The man beside her is her son-in-law, Stoker Vann. He's her sub-chief."

Tad remembered the name. Coach Kramer had admired his fast-ball in regional competition. Tad wondered if the young father still played baseball. Stoker Vann's mother-in-law was a small woman, but her voice carried throughout the church.

"Welcome to *Gateo UnalasDeske*," she began.

"Stomp and singing ground and ball field," Linda translated.

Nina Jumper continued. "The Snowbird Cherokee welcomes all people here to enjoy all we have planned. We offer fellowship to our kin East and West, and all who meet here. I thank Pastor Tim for this place to talk over things that are weighing on our hearts. Pastor, will you help us pray for the safe return of Rising Fawn Reed?"

Everyone seemed surprised, including Swimmer Reed himself, who was at the meeting with his younger children, but without his wife and oldest daughter. The two boys and three girls looked to their father, and seemed relieved when he did not object.

Pastor Tim took Nina Jumper's hand and held it high as he offered a prayer.

"Creator, we have talked with you inside these walls many times. We have called you by many names—Above Being, God our Father, Jesus Christ. You know the Snowbird Cherokee, both traditional and adaptive members of this great people.

106

They have lost one of their own: a dancer, a teacher, one who comforts the grieving, who brightens our days with her beautiful shawl and flying feet. Keep her safe until she returns to us, Creator."

"Amen," answered some. "Praise God" and "Thank you, Jesus," said others. Standing along the church's west wall, Tad saw Dora Tanner wipe her eyes with a lacy-edged handkerchief. Her husband shouted "hear, hear!" among the amens. Tad wondered how deeply the Atlanta couple wished for Rising Fawn's return. She had left behind her beautiful shawl, after all.

The Festival chief thanked Pastor Tim and faced the congregation, turning slowly on her heel until she made eye contact with everyone around the circle.

"This is a good place. Please play and sing and dance. But do everything in the manner acceptable to the values you hold in your church denominations.

"Some people may think this is a place for certain things, intoxicants like alcohol. We do not allow these things here. The people we have chosen to watch for this, please be vigilant. If you choose to use intoxicants, you will be asked to leave.

"That is all I have to say. Now my son-in-law will say some things," she concluded, transferring the baby from the young father's lap to her own.

If he didn't have her grace and serenity, Stoker Vann displayed a shy, earnest leadership as he rifled through his notes, then raised his laughing eyes to the congregation. "The town authorities have asked us to watch our fires carefully," he began. "We all know there has been some trouble lately, and our big turnout causes them concern."

He stopped, looked over the crowd, then nodded toward a back row. Ella Kituhwa stood, her sore arm resting in a yellow calico fabric sling. "The north campground is especially dry," she said.

"*Wa to*, Ella," Stoker thanked Linda's cousin.

Silence followed. Tad leaned toward Linda. "What's going on?" he whispered.

"He waits for other comments."

Satisfied, Stoker crammed one of his notes into the pocket of his jeans, then went on to the next. He talked about the upkeep of the facilities, then of schedule changes in the night's program. He had a strong, even voice, and was so patient with comments that even a few guest children from a Western Cherokee band spoke up, asking that a lower height table be used to display cornbread and sweets. Stoker took their request as seriously as any other, first complimenting the people who had brought the treats that delighted the children, a gospel singing trio from Tennessee.

Linda's earring skimmed Tad's shoulder. "Is this very boring to you?" she asked.

"Boring? Remember our gripe sessions at the dig site last summer? We could have used Stoker Vann and his mother-in-law to move things along."

Linda squeezed his arm, right in watchful sight lines of her family.

Stoker Vann was down to his last sheet of notepaper when his baby nodded off on Nina Jumper's shoulder. "Ned Socowah was called away to his cabin up on Deep Gap this morning. We are looking for a volunteer to hike up and bring Ned and his sister Shirley some festival food tonight."

Linda touched Tad's shoulder. "Could we do this, Tad?"

"Sure."

Linda looked to her parents, who nodded, then to Stoker Vann, who smiled and said, "Good, then."

Tad realized he welcomed both the opportunity to provide for their grim chaperone and take a walk with Linda in the moonlight.

The young sub-chief then had a quick private conference with Chief Nina before calling on the crowds attention again. "We have been asked to air out some talk about our minds' direction on the casino debate," he said in his strong, clear voice, slightly changed by what Tad thought was a wisp of uncertainty. "My daughter and the other babies have been lulled into their naps by our talk of showers and dessert tables, so let us honor them by keeping this talk as soft."

There were a few titters from his audience before Stoker Vann continued. "I will sit now. William Joyce and Swimmer Van will present their positions on this question."

Tad watched Rising Fawn's father and an imposing red-haired man enter the empty square in the middle of the church.

"Who's that?" Tad asked Linda.

"Mr. Joyce is a member of the bear clan."

"That guy's a Cherokee?"

"Some say his people were Five Dollar Indians—white people who got themselves listed on the Cherokee rolls back in the last century when Indian land was coming up for sale. But he is a clan member, yes."

"Let me guess—he thinks casinos are a good idea?"

"Well, yes."

The two men could not have been more different. William Joyce had a friendly, casual air, as open as the collar of his expensive, fringed shirt. Swimmer Reed looked at nothing but his bible, stuck with post-it notes in its pages.

When William Joyce held out his hand, Swimmer Reed seemed reluctant to take it in greeting. William Joyce made a small bow before their chief, then spoke to her and the assembly in a booming voice. "Perhaps Mr. Reed is too burdened by personal worry to represent a side in this complicated issue."

Swimmer Reed's head shot up from his bible. "I am eager to speak because of what has happened in my family. I have a wife who has disobeyed me and a daughter who has run away. That is what happens when we let in the corruption of the outside world," he declared.

Tad sat more upright. Maybe it was time to be suspicious of more people than the Tanners. He turned to Linda, who looked sad. He needed to listen more as possibilities developed in the back of his mind.

William Joyce spoke next. "There are many who don't view the casino as outside corruption. Some think it is a means to work our way out of poverty. The Cow Creek band, with little hope and few jobs, now have a springboard to prosperity, because of a casino. The Tulalip opened theirs last year. Leaders wanted jobs for one hundred Indians. Now its success makes three hundred jobs. Eighty-one of us lost our employment when the Aurora toy factory closed down. One lost his life."

After a moment of silence, William Joyce left his center position. Swimmer

Reed stepped forward. "My fellow Cherokee speaks of jobs and prosperity. I say, how many more lives will be lost if we go his way? Those of us who follow the same Christian faith as our white neighbors consider ourselves spiritual equals. We agree with them in their opposition. How can anything but evil come of vice?"

Mr. Joyce stood taller. "None of our people need to gamble."

"And do you think that none will?"

Others joined the two men's debate. The Fundamentalist Christians backed Swimmer Reed. Some of the traditional Cherokee agreed with his position too, saying that temptation to gamble would be too great. Others thought the bingo parlor they now ran was a harmless diversion. Still others took a hard line against both bingo and the casino, saying that gambling was wrong. Tad found himself pulling out of their quiet, respectful argument and watched individuals.

But soon Linda touched his arm. "I have to prepare to dance," she said.

Chapter Twelve

Linda faced the ragged man. His long, stringy blond hair fell into his unshaven face. He weaved in closer, blocking her path.

"So the other little butterfly flew away? Or did her wings get singed?

Linda could not find her voice. The exhilaration that came with demonstrating her dance, even without Rising Fawn beside her, evaporated, leaving her feeling alone and afraid.

Then she realized that she was not alone. Tad took the man's shoulder gently but firmly. "Do you know something about Rising Fawn's disappearance, sir?" he asked as he placed Linda out of the man's reach.

"I know what I hear. That daddy of hers wanted to clip her wings. So she ran away. Maybe she got burnt. I got burnt, did you know?"

Pastor Tim stood behind the man now. "This is Bill Chasteen. He's been living in the church's basement since his home burned down. Bill this is Tad and Linda.

"Cellar! It's noting but a damp dark cellar."

"But it's where you need to stay one hour after your medication, remember?" Pastor Tim kept a firm hold on the man's arm.

"I wanted to see the butterfly dance."

"I know."

He reached for Linda. "I will feel bad about scaring you, little butterfly. In an hour." His voice got quieter. "I'm having a bad time, you know? My mama left me that house. I got no money to rebuild. I chop wood for folks. Hear all the disagreements. Not in tune with Harmony Festival, is it?"

"No, sir," Linda agreed.

"Pastor Tim turned the man around. "I'll walk you back to the church, Bill."

"Just for an hour?"

"That's all. You'll feel much better soon."

Linda felt Tad's light hold as they watched the two men make their way away from the dance tent and toward the church. What did she do to her grandmother's wonderful gift of her shawl? Had she infused it with her own fear? Fear of someone sick and harmless? She shivered. Tad held her closer.

Soon they were joined by members of her audience. The children came first, running their faces through the long fringe of her shawl. They traced Grandmother

Longknife's rose and vine beadwork with their fingers. The adults followed, praising her dance, asking her to demonstrate her rattles. Tad stood back, smiling, looking proud. Linda found her peace again in his light eyes.

It was six o'clock before they gathered food from each booth to pack and bring up the mountain to her chaperone and his sister. Linda looked forward to having Tad to herself on a quiet hike. She needed to sort through her thoughts with someone she loved and trusted. She thanked Cousin Ella for her full thermos of corn soup and placed it in her canvas knapsack.

"That's it," Tad proclaimed. "We can go."

As they trekked through the north campground the air became fragrant with honeysuckle. They passed people at their campsites, enjoying their dinners.

"Will we miss the social dancing?" Tad asked.

"Only the Buffalo Dance. It starts at dusk. The rest doesn't start until nine or so. Don't worry, Ned Socowah's cabin is only an hour's hike for a fit baseball player," she teased.

Tad grinned as he lifted the pack higher on his shoulder. Such little things pleased him, put joy in his step, Linda realized. The thought made her smile, and she gave thanks for the gift of her friend.

"Tell me about the Buffalo dance?" he asked.

"Well, long ago, the Cherokee did the dance at this time of day because that's when the buffalo were bedding down. Its song is a lullaby to sing them to sleep, then a prayer of thanks and apology to all the animals, promising we will take only what we need, and use it all."

"What are the words?" Tad asked.

"We do not know them anymore," Linda said sadly. "It's so old we don't remember. But we do the dance. We can keep that alive."

"And the social dancing? You're sure I'll be able to catch on? There's no hoops or flying shawls or anything?"

Linda laughed. It felt good. "There are only four steps, Tad, and we dance in lines. It is not hard."

Linda spotted a familiar level rock. "We are about halfway to the cabin. Maybe we should rest here."

"Sure."

She eased her backpack from her shoulders. "You are very agreeable."

"I'm in very agreeable company."

They sat together on the rock, which was warm from being in the shining sunlight all afternoon. From it, they could see down to the burning campfires of Harmony Festival.

"It was not always so today," Linda reminded him. "Sheriff Harrison was not friendly or patient with us. Neither was Swimmer Reed or Bill Chasteen." An involuntary shiver ran down her arms at the mention of the homeless man.

"Sounds like we're starting to consider suspects, Nancy Drew."

"I suppose we are." Linda felt a bone-aching weariness.

"Let's assume it's someone she knows."

"Sheriff Harrison thinks she's run away with Jim Greene."

He winced. "Let's consider others."

"Why?"

"Remember those pictures of missing kids they used to put on everything from milk cartons to grocery bags?"

"Yes?"

"It came out that most of them were taken by their own fathers or mothers or grandparents locked in custody or visitation battles."

"But Rising Fawn is not a child."

"Sure, but she's in a volatile state with her parents over Jim Greene."

"That's true. But Tad, Peggy Reed went to the police station with us."

"But Swimmer Reed would not. Then went on to debate the gambling issue and called his wife and daughter disobedient."

"Maybe he only believes as Sheriff Harrison does, that my friend has run off."

"And maybe he knows exactly where she is. Does Rising Fawn have any other relatives? Ones not here at the festival?"

"An aunt. Her father's sister works for the government in Washington. She is helping create a museum of the American Indian."

"Would she keep Rising Fawn with her, if her brother asked?"

"I don't think so! Swimmer Reed does not approve of his independent sister and her city life among the government bureaucrats! That's the last place he might send his daughter."

"Dead end, then. Anyone else?"

"Tad, Rising Fawn's father may be unyielding, but he is not a bad man. That's why my friend is so torn. Her father loves her, and his family. Do you think he would risk worrying Peggy?"

"Maybe for a few days he might think it was worth it. If they got their daughter back. Let's keep our eyes on Swimmer Reed."

"All right," she agreed.

She found herself almost hoping that Rising Fawn was being hidden for a little while by her father. She would miss the festival and dancing, but she would be safe.

"You try one," Tad prodded.

"A suspect?" she asked uneasily.

"Linda, I know this is hard for you—"

"The Tanners."

"What?"

"The couple from Atlanta."

"I know who you mean, but why?"

"Rising Fawn's fancy shawl. Their eyes are greedy for it."

"Oh. Oh, no."

"I know it's not a very strong reason."

"It's enough. We should keep an eye on them. I'm just dreading the job."

"Not me. Why do they see my family as competitors? I think they might be as bad to the Snowbird people as that thief Jackson!"

Tad winced. "Andrew Jackson?"

"Of course Andrew Jackson. Treaty breaker. Indian killer."

"Good. You watch the Tanners. Just let them keep their hair, will you?"

She laughed. "Your turn, Buffalo Man."

Tad heaved a small sigh. He'd done that before, she remembered. When he was going to say something unpleasant. "Okay. I'll jump into the fire of your political debate to come up with another possibility. Swimmer Reed pressed on with showing up at the debate this afternoon. As I watched Mr. Reed and William Joyce present their arguments, I couldn't help but notice they looked a little, well, uneven in their presentations."

"Why? Because William Joyce is rich and better dressed and educated? Because he talks and looks more like you?"

Tad winced. "I knew I shouldn't be bringing this up while you were still out to murder Andrew Jackson."

"Wait. If Swimmer Reed is worried about his daughter, that would make him distracted, not as good a debate partner. And he did not quote scripture once, though he held his bible in his hand."

"Full of post-it notes at the ready. for quoting passages. Now, who would benefit from his worry and distraction?"

Linda felt herself warm with embarrassment. "William Joyce. He has offered his pool hall for conversion into a casino."

"Bingo."

"He already runs the bingo parlor. And a store that sells Indian trinkets that are made in China. He wants to be a millionaire before he's thirty."

"How old is he?"

"Twenty-nine. That is a powerful motive, isn't it, Tad? He would have a lot to gain by keeping Swimmer Reed unsettled," Linda said, feeling more than a little unsettled herself. She did not like thinking of her friends and neighbors in this way.

"So, we have another suspect to keep an eye on. Does it exhaust you?"

"I exhaust myself. With doubting you. Oh, Tad I'm sorry."

"Forget it."

"I cannot forget it." She also could not look at him, until she felt a gentle poke at her elbow.

"Hey. I'm just glad you don't think I'm ugly."

"Ugly?"

He pointed politely, like a Cherokee, with his chin, in the direction of the festival grounds below. 'Skinny *genvsge like knasgowa*.' I think that's the general consensus when I walk by."

"Legs like the heron? Is that what they say?"

"They don't know I've learned a few words from you and your folks, I guess."

Linda giggled.

"What are you laughing at? That's harsh, Ahyoka!"

"The heron has very sturdy legs," she tried.

"Aw, you don't have to sweet talk me."

Blue misting clouds were settling over their resting spot. "Tad, Rising Fawn and I used to meet here on this rock when were children on the first night of Harmony Festival."

He lifted the hair off her shoulder and sifted it through his fingers. "I liked Rising Fawn right away, Linda. Even more, I liked the way you two smiled and giggled like

121

kids when you were with her. I was getting a peek at what I missed, the time when you were a little girl."

"Tad Gist, you are making me cry."

His eyes widened. "Don't tell Guli on me. I'm already on probation with him."

"I won't," she promised softly, then looked up at the sky. "Creator," she prayed, "my friend Rising Fawn and I used to call this place Second Heaven, because we felt closer to you here. We were above the tops of trees, First Heaven. We are now in the clouds again, two steps off the earth. So I ask the angels of this place to keep my friend safe where she sleeps tonight, safe and knowing in one corner of her heart, that Taddeusz, your courageous one, and I are looking for her, are working to bring her home."

Chapter Thirteen

Ned Socowah's place was set well off the road and deep in the blue mist where Linda had said her beautiful prayer. Tad was beginning to understand how this blue mist was such an important part of Linda's homeland. He was glad to follow its swirling, disappearing patterns, to feel its coolness as it dampened his clothes and skin. After Linda's prayer on the rock, it was easy to imagine that they were climbing up through the Cherokee heavens.

Behind the rough-hewed cabin, Tad made out the dim shapes of other structures.

"That's an old blacksmith shop that Ned uses to work on his healing concoctions," Linda explained. "Beyond it are a root cellar and a corncrib that he uses to shelter—"

A sorrowful bleat and tinkling bells interrupted her. "Goats," she finished.

Tad followed as she strode past the cabin toward the sounds. Tad had only seen goats at a game farm he visited as a kid. He remembered them chewing his sleeve and shoelaces. He caught up to Linda as she discovered the animal tied to a metal stake in the ground. The animal they found looked more like a sheep, with long white hair and a head that almost reached Linda's shoulder. Linda came closer, talking softly in Cherokee. It worked. The pitiful bleating stopped. Linda stooped and ran her hand down the goat's leg. Tad saw that the soft hair that grew over the legs had been shaved from the goat's left hind one.

A screen door slammed. Tad turned to see Ned Socowah. "*Thu :thi*?" he called out.

"*Ha yu*," Linda answered in a reassuring tone as she rose back to her feet. "It is Ahyoka Tassel and Tad Gist, Mr. Socowah. We have brought you and Shirley some supper from the festival."

The big man's stance seemed to ease as he left his porch and joined them. He hitched his thumbs in his jeans' belt loops as he regarded them. "Leg infection. I had to shave around it."

"Did you use comfrey in the salve? Like you helped me?"

"Comfrey, yes. And plantain, and wild geranium."

"Remember I told you how Ned helped me when I hurt myself, Tad?"

"Sure."

"She's almost better," Ned said now. "Just lonesome." He released the goat from her chain. "Come inside," he said. But his eyes narrowed before he turned. Tad wondered if he was still doing his chaperone job. Or maybe he was just worried about setting his goat free.

As they approached the porch, Tad saw a shadow move away from the gingham curtains at the window. But when they entered the spare, tidy hearth room, only its ticking, banjo box clock greeted them. Linda and Tad settled their backpacks on the square wooden table. Together they emptied them of food containers. At the deep kitchen sink, Tad noticed a pile of what he now knew were ramps, the wild onion that mountain people prized. There were greens on a cutting board too, and six peeled potatoes and one half-peeled.

"Is Shirley at home, Mr. Socowah?" Linda asked.

Their chaperone ran his hand through his closely cropped black hair. "She was just here," he said.

Linda scanned the hallway that led into the large front room. There was a yellow light coming from under the first door. "May I?" she asked.

Ned shrugged, but Tad sensed there was encouragement in his stance.

Linda approached the door, but before she got to it, a woman who Tad guessed to be about a decade younger than Ned, maybe in her mid-twenties, came out, holding a kerosene lamp. Her hair was pulled back from her face and hung over her shoulder in a single long braid that reached her waist. She wore a dark skirt and muslin blouse with delicate embroidered flowers sewed into its scooped neckline. There was something as fragile as those flowers in her smile, Tad thought.

"Ahyoka. *Hi qina lii*," she said into the quiet stillness between them.

"*Wa to*," Linda thanked her softly, then looked toward Tad. "*Agi-nalii*, Tad," she introduced him.

Tad saw an amused look start at the corner of the young woman's mouth. "Tadpole?" she whispered.

It was the same mistake Linda had made when first hearing his name, thinking he'd been named for an earlier stage of a frog. Tad grimaced and rolled his eyes, trying to make Linda's friend's smile widen.

Linda switched to English. "Taddeusz. It means 'he has courage.'"

"Oh?" Shirley's dark eyes went wide. "And does this one have much courage in him?" Her mouth was sober, but her yes were still laughing. Seeing him as a baby frog, maybe. No, it was something else. Something making Linda blush and giggle behind her hand.

Tad looked at Ned Socowah for a clue, but he was staring at Linda and his sister with a look of wonder.

Shirley gave Ned her lamp. "Put it on the hearth. I will light another." She turned to her guests. "Please excuse my brother. He has been living by himself for a long time and forgets his manners."

"I let them in," Ned defended himself, placing her lamp on the mantel above the stone hearth.

"And with the water already boiling, you did not think to offer coffee?" She looked to Tad and Linda. "You will stay for coffee?"

"Yes," Linda answered for them. "We brought festival food." She looked to the sink. "Shall we two finish your soup so you will have two meals prepared?"

"Good! Sit, sit," she encouraged her guests. "All the chairs of this house have not been filled since—well, for a long time."

Shirley reached behind the kitchen sink for a box of wooden matches. She brought them to the table where there was a blue glass kerosene lamp. She struck a match. But her hand shook as she tried to light it. She stared at her hand until the wooden match burned down to her fingers. She dropped it, startled.

"I will do it," her brother offered.

"The screaming. Did you hear it?"

Linda reached across the table. She took Shirley's hand. "Let's listen together," she said.

Tad held his breath. Linda was doing the same, with her eyes closed.

127

Ned Socowah looked out the window.

"Do you hear it now?" Shirley asked.

"No," Linda whispered.

"Neither do I."

Linda released her hand. Ned took three long strides to the stove. He grabbed the coffee pot from the back burner and brought it to the table. "There. Coffee," he declared.

"Ned does not hear the screams," his sister said.

He turned his back and rifled into his cupboard. "My sister lived in town. She is not used to night sounds. Animals, the wind."

"I know loneliness.   And fear. The screaming has both."

Ned slammed four coffee cups on the table. "It was not my idea to leave you to collect these two. You said you wanted to try a time without me."

Her voice became smaller. "The storm."

"I phoned Alice Glory to send someone to look in on you. But the road was washed out."

"I know. I know," she whispered, looking down at her hands.

"She has been hearing these screams," Ned explained quietly to Linda and Tad.

His sister sighed. "And now Ned cannot return to the festival. Because there is so little harmony here, in me." She turned to her guests. "Are they the echoes of my own cries for the one who was lost? Is that what I hear?"

"What do they know? They are outsiders," her brother scolded.

Tad caught a flash of hurt in Linda's eyes. But she went to the sink, and began chopping ramps. Even in that sad house, Tad felt his mouth watering as the sharp, pungent odor was released.

"Well, there is very little harmony at the festival this year, too," Linda said matter-of-factly as she worked. "I had to do the Fancy Shawl Dance demonstrations alone, because Rising Fawn is missing from this morning."

"Where did she go?" Shirley asked.

"No one knows."

Shirley pulled out a big cast iron frying pan from a drawer near the stove. "Do you fry ramps in pork fat?" she asked.

"Just a piece of fat, the size of your thumb," Linda answered.

"Yes, that is best," Shirley agreed. "What are they saying about Rising Fawn?" she asked. Without any of her former difficulty she lit a burner.

Tad looked up at the brother, whose face reflected his own puzzlement. Linda went on with her chopping, then began to rinse some pole beans. "Some say Rising Fawn went off with Jim Greene because he was there, because she argued with her father about him."

"Jim Greene brought down a fine buck last Fall, and shared venison with us in a dark time," Shirley said softly. "He wants to marry Rising Fawn, I think."

"Yes. But she promised to dance with us."

"He is respectful, Ahyoka. Jim Greene would not keep Rising Fawn from dancing."

"That is what I think, too."

"But her father does not think this way?"

"No. He tries to put his daughter out of his mind, maybe. He argues against the casino with William Joyce."

"At Harmony Festival? Such talk? About the gambling?"

"Yes."

The young woman shook her head. "They should all leave the festival grounds for that talk. They should leave, like Rising Fawn."

"Tad and I, we do not think she left."

"I do not understand you, Ahyoka. You said that she is gone."

"We think someone took her."

Shirley stopped stirring the piled high greens in the frying pan. Her hands shook again.

"You trouble my sister, Linda Tassel," Ned said, rising from his chair to face her. "Rising Fawn ran off. She showed disrespect for her elders."

His sister stood between them. "Her father can be hard, I think. People say—"

"You don't know what people say anymore, sister. And your ears are not good."

"Because they hear pain? Because I have not learned to harden my heart against the pain?" she challenged.

"Did I leave you in that place?" he demanded. "Did I forget I had a sister?"

Shirley turned off the burner, then away from the stove. "I am so tired, Ned," she whispered. Tears wet her cheeks.

He took her arm and led her toward the bedroom. Linda left the cutting board and rushed after them. "Shirley! I'm sorry, I did not mean—"

The young widow reached out and touched Linda's face. "It was good of you to come, Ahyoka," she said. "Go back down with your brave friend and dance." She smiled sadly at Tad. "You both have too much life for this place."

Chapter Fourteen

"I did not mean to make her cry."

"You didn't. You were doing great," Tad said, reaching for Linda's hand. "She was a different person when the two of you were cooking."

"I knew a different person. Shirley was always so full of life, so funny. I wanted her back. I thought doing something together, something we always did at festival time, might help."

"It did."

"But now she is crying. And her brother is angry with me."

"With us. He named us both outsiders."

"Should we go?"

Tad scanned the room. What was he seeing, Linda wondered. That the small cabin was a sad place. Did he regret coming? The festival promised dancing and escape from the young widow who heard screams that others did not. "Let's finish the soup first. Together," he suggested.

Linda smiled. "All right."

"We can leave it as an offering to our chaperone. I don't think he approves of me yet."

Linda began by transferring the ramps from the frying pan to the soup pot. "Ned has been living up here, alone, for many years, since he got out of the marines. He was hurt in that bombing that killed all those American service people in Beirut back in '83."

"The peacekeepers."

"Yes, the peacekeepers, from many nations. He was wild when he first came home, full of heart sickness because so many of his friends were killed all around him.

"He built this place and did not come down to town much. But we went to him when we needed healing, after he started working with the plants. Shirley was proud of her big brother. After she married, her husband helped her bring him down off the mountain and work in the community again. They were volunteer firefighters together. When Shirley lost her husband and became sad and still, Ned brought her here."

"So I guess he's got bigger things to worry about than chaperoning us at Harmony Festival."

Linda locked her fingers with his as he handed her the coffee mug. She kissed his cheek and he smiled at her in that way that melted her heart. A slight redness flushed his face.

"Let's finish here so we can head down the mountain and dance," she suggested.

His grin widened.

Linda filled the dishpan with soapy water and washed the utensils. Tad finished clearing the table. As they worked together, Linda's sadness for Shirley mingled with her worry for Rising Fawn. From the bedroom, the sounds of Shirley's weeping became louder, and her brother's pleas more desperate.

As she worked at the sink, Linda fought through her fear and found the words to a song they all sang when children. Soon she felt Tad's hand at the small of her back. She thought he would ask for a translation.

"Louder," he urged, tilting his head toward the bedroom door. "Sing it louder."

She did, through the next four verses. She finished the song as water flowed down the drain. Tad handed her the dish towel, kissing her temple. Linda realized the cabin was perfectly silent.

"Now tell me what all of that meant," he asked quietly.

"It is a prayer, to gain serenity. Our mothers sang it to us on festival nights when we had trouble dropping off to sleep. The verses take us through all the heavens."

"All the heavens?"

"Yes. Seven."

"So, that flat rock was just the second rest stop on a long way up?" he teased. Metaphysical teasing, Linda realized, from a person not of the Tsa la ki. Teasing that did not mock, or belittle.

"Yes," she told him. "'Let my soul be in the first heaven,' I began the song."

"The tops of the trees."

"Very good. And then, the second."

"The clouds."

"You remembered."

"What are the rest?"

"Our third heaven is as high as the moon. The fourth: the sun, the fifth the planets, the sixth, the constellations."

"And, the seventh?"

"The seventh is where the Creator lives."

Ned Socowah came out of his sister's bedroom. "She is drifting off toward Neptune, I think," he said quietly. "*Wa to,* Ahyoka."

"We are sorry for your trouble, sir." Linda watched Ned's face, hoping to see signs of the gift of serenity he wanted so badly to give his sister.

"Shirley was almost herself with you, for a little while. She was joking," he said.

"Yes, she was."

"She has not been that well in a long time."

He opened his clenched hand and Linda saw a brown prescription bottle. "They are to help her sleep. She needed none tonight, because of your song."

"You know that song, Ned?"

"Yes. I try to find other ways, our ways. I do not want anyone taking her to a hospital." He bowed his head until Linda could only see the spiral whirl of his hair. "I want my sister returned. As herself, not someone like me. I will do anything. Ahyoka, I am treating her decent."

"Of course you are, Ned."

"But I will do anything. You understand?"

"Yes," she said, though she was not sure she did.

The intense emotion left his face. His hard, formal mask was back. "Thank you for coming, and for the food. I will have it ready and hot for her when she wakes."

Without the festival food as a burden, their load was an easy one on the way down the mountain, but Linda didn't feel any lighter. Their visit with Ned and Shirley was more disturbing than she could understand. She wanted to talk with Tad about it, but didn't know how. Her thoughts were as cloudy as the blue mist that clung to her mountains.

"Linda?"

"Yes?"

"Why was Mr. Socowah so determined to let you know he was taking care of his sister?"

"I don't know, Tad."

"Was it strange to you?"

136

"Maybe it was because I saw the medicine."

"Yeah. He was apologizing to you for using the medicine. Is that what it seemed like?"

"Yes."

"But he didn't use it."

"Not this time. Ned is a traditionalist, an herb doctor himself. He must have been very desperate to turn to Western medicine for his sister's care."

"Yeah, I guess that makes sense. Hey, what was the joke?"

"Joke?"

"Between you and Shirley. You all got it but me."

"Well, it is hard to translate."

"Translate? You were all speaking English!"

"Were we?"

"Sure! Don't you remember? She thought I was named for a tadpole, then you said no, Taddeusz meant courageous, and she asked if I had courage in me and you both laughed and...hey, you do remember!" he accused her suddenly. "You just don't want to tell me!"

It must have been his Irish blood that enabled him to see into her heart, and past her evasion, Linda decided. "Well, it was a little naughty."

"Naughty?"

"Only a little. Do you hear the dance music down there? They have already started. We'd better hurry."

He stopped and took her arms, holding her so close their noses were almost touching. "Tell me," he demanded.

"I am getting to it."

"Linda! You're blushing!"

"White people blush. I get warm sometimes, that's all. All right, then. There is an older meaning of courage. A meaning the people of these mountains still use. Shirley was asking me if I found you...you know, sexy."

Tad threw back his head and laughed. Linda took advantage of his loosened hold on her to slip under his arm and power walk toward the campground below.

"Hey, wait!" he called after her. "What did you answer?"

"I did not answer her, remember?" she called back, giggling.

Chapter Fifteen

Tad watched Guli circle the fire. Around him people came close in eager anticipation. Colorful quilts were draped over benches around the fire pit. The Harmony Festival's participants still wore their casual dress, now with a sweater or jacket to keep off the night's chill. About half the men sported a variety of hats—baseball caps with teams or farming equipment logos on them, cowboy hats in felt and straw, and a few fedoras, like the one Tad held in this hand. It was a gift from when he and Linda worked at the archeological dig last summer.

Beside Tad, Theda Longknife nodded to the pulsing drumbeat as she sat in her wheelchair. The rest of her family joined the opening dance, which was forming two lines. James Tassel entered the men's line that was beginning to snake around another, made up of women and girls. He settled behind Guli and his group of young men. Harry Longknife joined towards the end of the line. Three generations of Longknife women took corresponding age-based positions in their line. Linda wore a gauzy purple skirt over a black body suit. A red kerchief wound around her head. Her turtle shell rattles were tied with leather thongs around her ankles.

"Guli Whitepath," Theda said in a soft, disapproving tone, "why so soon for a friendship dance?"

"That's not the usual order?" Tad asked her.

"Only if he is trying to test a certain young suitor."

"Oh, I'm used to that," Tad said, trying to sound more confident than he felt as he hung his hat off the arm of the wheelchair. Just what he needed. Another challenge.

"Watch a little while," Aunt Theda advised, now softly tapping out the beat on Tad's arm. "Then join behind the last young man, and follow."

The man Theda said was the Dance Chief gave Guli a hand signal. Guli began to sing. His voice was pure and direct, and put new life into the dancers' steps. Linda's turtle rattles helped quicken the women's inside circle in response.

Theda's voice became wistful. "Our Ahyoka oils her shells well before a dance. They make just the right tone."

"Did you teach her that?"

"I did. And how to tie properly, Some women tie so tightly that by the time they are around the circle two or three times they cut off circulation. I watch for that—

140

blue legs. Then I call them over, show them how to tie where their muscles are. That way, when they stomp, the calf muscle shakes the shells."

"Did you dance yourself, Miss Longknife?"

"Oh, yes! With evaporated milk cans when I was little. It was fun, even the practicing. Now Ahyoka wears my turtles. I used cotton wadding for under the turtles. It was good, but Ahyoka found better—foam rubber pads, see them? My niece is very clever." Her fingers closed around Tad's arm. "But you know that."

"Yes."

"And full of beauty. Join the dance now, before one of those Big Cove boys get the idea that you do not care for her."

Tad only hesitated when he caught the scent of Dora Tanner's gardenia perfume.

But Linda's aunt chuckled. "They won't stay by me long."

"I'm not leaving you with them."

Theda Longknife sighed now. "Then watch. And learn."

"So nice to see you out tonight Tad, Miss Longknife!" Breman Tanner greeted them as his wife tried to wipe the dancer's dust from her rhinestone studded skirt.

Then something caught her eye. "Oh, those drums. Look, the orange ochre shade of that one matches a sand painting that

141

dear old Navajo, or was he Hopi, did for us in Arizona last winter."

"What does the song mean, Miss Longknife?" her husband asked.

Tad watched Linda's aunt's face grow solemn. "Oh, the words are very old, so no one is sure. But my grandfather used to tell folks they mean 'grab yourself a white man and throw him on the fire.'"

"Oh. Oh, my," Dora Tanner exclaimed before a smile found its way to her face. "Breman, I do believe we are too close to those dust clouds to remain tidy."

"We'll head for a higher level then," her husband readily agreed, as he touched the rim of his designer cowboy hat. "Miss Longknife, Tad," he said politely before taking his wife's arm and leading her away.

Tad knelt and hid his laughter behind the arm of the wheelchair. Aunt Theda ruffled his hair. "I can still hold my own with that kind of Anglo," she declared. "Now go and dance. And take your hat!"

She snatched up his battered felt fedora and placed it on his head.

"Why do I need my hat?"

"Claim her with it."

"How?"

Just then a young Cherokee let out a whoop when his place in the men's circle corresponded with Linda's in hers. He was a good-looking guy with two feathers attached to his shoulder-length hair. He lunged for Linda, but she was too fast and eluded his grasp, even with the turtle shells tied to her limbs.

"Hey, what kind of a dance—"

"Go!" Theda pushed him forward.

Tad took his place behind the young men as the dance continued. The stomping step came easily to him, but he couldn't seem to work his way closer to Linda. She slipped away from the grasp of another dancer and moved her section of the women's line faster. Corresponding movements started throughout the double rings of dancers. James Tassel spun his Naomi into a neat double twirl and entwined her in his woven sash belt. Guli covered the shoulders of a beaming girl with his jacket. Linda's grandparents shared a squeeze and a colorful handkerchief between them.

The whoops grew louder, the music faster paced. The heat, sweat, and dust flew, Tad heard the clear, oiled tuned rattle shells approaching. He reached out his hand, caught a waist. Hers. He reeled her in.

"Ahyoka," he gasped out, not believing his good luck.

Linda laughed.

Tad grabbed the hat off his head and planted it on hers. The final hoop went up into the night sky as the dancers, all couples now, burst forward out into the night air.

Linda was still catching her breath as they collapsed together on the bank of a hill overlooking the dance ground. Tad released her leggings from her calves.

"Massage?" he offered.

"Oh, Tad, that is just what I need!"

He heard the exhaustion in her voice. He helped her slip her feet out of her moccasins and went to work, beginning on her calloused heels. His thumbs felt for muscles, His fingers worked the knotted tightness. Linda nodded and made encouraging sounds as he worked. Then she stretched out her legs, right down to fanning out her toes, before smiling at him from under the rim of his fedora.

Tad grinned. "So. You've got my hat. I've got your turtle leggings. Are we married?"

She threw his hat at him and muttered a Cherokee phrase he doubted she'd ever translate. "That was a friendship dance. Marriage is much more serious."

"What do you call fighting my way through Guli, clouds of dust, and all your boyfriends?"

She grinned. "Smart."

He grunted. "Besides, we've done serious things together too."

Her fingers wove through the dewy grass and found his. "Yes," she agreed.

144

"We have. We are together in a serious thing now, Taddeusz."

"Any more ideas?" he asked her.

"Maybe Peggy would let me go through Rising Fawn's belongings? For a name, a phone number? Maybe she left something behind that would help us get in touch with Jim Greene? Do you think she would allow that, Tad?"

"We should ask," he agreed, sitting up.

Linda was already standing. Tad."

"Yes?"

"Something is wrong."

He heard the fear in her voice so lost no time in scrambling to his feet. "What do you see?"

She nodded toward the north. "Too much smoke for campfires. Oh, Tad, I think—"

She didn't finish before screams and shouts of "Fire!" began.

Chapter Sixteen

Linda's heart was racing from their run.

She and Tad stopped at the edge of the crowd of people listening to Harmony Festival Chief Nina Jumper's clear, calm instructions. "Children, their caregivers and vehicles will move to the south campground. We will wait for word from the firefighters there."

She nodded to her son-in-law. Stoker Vann stepped forward. "For those staying here, we need shovels and buckets and able bodies," he declared in a clear calm voice. "Ned Socowah's got a hose on the fire already. We'll try and hold it until the pumper gets here."

Someone put a shovel into Tad's hand. He turned and gave Linda a quick hug before he jumped on the back of a truck with the rest of the men.

"Ahyoka! we need you here," her mother called.

Soon her parents' specially equipped van was loaded with children. She secured the wheelchair before putting the last of the toddlers into her aunt's waiting arms. Aunt

Theda looked pleased. Linda hesitated as she touched her grandmother's shoulder.

"You have a request, Ahyoka?" Her grandmother was good at reading faces.

"Yes, Grandmother."

"Bring it to the festival *uku*. She is our driver. Aunt Theda and her mother smiled. Matching sisters' smiles. Matching eyes bright with unshed tears.

Linda ran to the driver's side of the van. "This is the last of the children," she said.

"There is room for you," Chief Nina Jumper invited her.

"I want to stay, *Uku*, to help here."

The older woman nodded. "*O sta tsi ki,*" she approved, pulling Linda's bandana down off her forehead so that it covered her nose and mouth. "Wet it," she instructed. "And get the men around you to do the same, gentle Warrior Woman."

Linda watched the van pull away as the last of the elder women and children drove toward the south campground. She prayed that the winds would stay right to keep them safe.

Then she ran for her family's deserted camp space. She rifled through her grandmother's sewing supplies until she found a pair of scissors. Every bucket at the site had been confiscated by the firefighters, but she found a plastic cake saver that she hoped would hold water. She put the scissors inside then crammed the rest of the space with loose weave blouses left behind by her mother. She wondered where her father and Tad and Guli were.

Armed with her supplies she made her way to the creek.

Soon after she found soot-covered people on the bucket line leading up from the rushing waters. Ned Socowah led them, his fire-fighting experience evident. But he was the only one with a collar high enough to pull over his nose and mouth.

Linda went to work.

Despite some grousing resistance, she managed to cover the line with her makeshift, water-soaked face covering. There was hardly a slowdown from the campsite's water spigot to the smoky fire.

Next, Linda snaked her way among the men clearing debris and digging a fire line ring. She'd given out all the face masks she'd concocted from the blouses and started shredding the hemline of her long purple skirt before she found Tad.

When he grinned his teeth looked very white. "Tad!" she called out. Cover your mouth and nose!"

He leaned on his shovel. "Heard you were coming. And I like the color purple."

By the time the pumper from the Roaring Rock volunteer fire department made its way up to the camp grounds, the participants of Harmony Festival had done their work. The fire had destroyed four campsites and caused damage to two more. But the efforts of the buckets and Pastor Tim's garden hose brigades had combined with the fire line diggers to put the blaze out.

Linda watched Tad scan the weary assemblage. It was Saturday night at Harmony Festival, when they all would have listening to music and dancing. But this year most of the women and the children were at the south campground, waiting for the signal to make a safe return. The ones who had fought the fire stood around the burnt-out campsites, except for Ned Socowah, who had rushed back up the mountain to his sister. Sheriff Harrison questioned the families of the two men who had lost the most—Swimmer Reed and Joseph Mayes. The Roaring Rock firefighters picked through the ashes, making sure they were cold.

Fighting the fire had made them all— white and Cherokee look the same color, Linda realized, shaking her head.

Tad approached with a thermos and handed her a paper cup before filling it with cool water. "You have the strength to laugh?"

She took a long drink.

Stoker Vann approached. Tad ladled water into his cup. Stoker had worked very close to the blaze. When Linda had wrapped his face, she's noticed burn holes in his sleeve.

She laughed again.

"What is so funny?"

"Well, look at us," Linda. "All of us, the same. Not Eastern and Western Cherokee, not Appalachian gospel singers and town firemen. We're not even town or farm folks tonight."

Tad laughed, tugging at the purple remnant of her skirt that still dangled around his neck.

The young sub-chief nodded. "Yes, we're all Ahyoka's raccoons."

"Raccoon Guardians of the Earth, if you please," she insisted.

Sheriff Harrison approached. "I hear you're the boss man, Mr. Vann," he said.

Stoker Vann looked confused. "Boss? No."

"Well, who is?"

"We do not have bosses. But maybe you want to speak with my mother-in-law."

"What?"

"She is a who. Nina Jumper."

Harrison pushed his hat back off his brow. "The old lady with all the kids, where I came in? The one who badgered me with questions?"

"That would be her I think, yes."

"What does she have to do with anything?"

"I thought you were asking to speak with our leader?"

"I was!"

"She is Festival Chief." He straightened his loose posture. "Do you want me to get her?"

"Will you please tell me why you people talk in circles? And how you can't even take a compliment?"

"A compliment? I thought you were looking for somebody?"

"Somebody to congratulate on the effectiveness of your teamwork!"

"Teamwork needs a team."

"And a team needs people like you and Ned Socowah there on the front lines."

Stoker shrugged. "And direction from our leader. And people to keep the children safe and calm."

Harrison frowned. "Look. The fire's officially out. You've got the all-clear to resume your pow-wow. Understand?"

Stoker Vann's posture looked even more casual. "Sure. Thanks."

Stoker Vann's face did not break into a grin until he saw the back of the exasperated policeman. "I will tell my mother-in-law that you think she is a good leader."

That grin prevented Linda from keeping her own expression sober as Sheriff Harrison turned to her and Tad.

"Your friend show up yet?"

"No, sir."

"I'm sorry. Listen, I understand you two spotted the fire from a distance."

"Yes, sir," Tad answered for them.

"I've already questioned the first on the scene, the one who thought of that church garden hose. Ned Socowah. Good man. Firefighter himself. But he's always got to rush home to that sister of his. Now, did you two, from your perch above, notice anyone suspicious around the campsites before the fire started?"

They both answered no together. That's when the sheriff frowned, dismissed Tad, and escorted Linda beneath a large tulip poplar tree.

Linda watched Tad pull away from the circle of Cherokee men and fold his arms, watching. The gesture comforted her as she turned to face Sheriff Harrison and his questions.

"One of those burned-out tents belongs to the family of the young woman you were looking for, I understand. Strictly traditional folks. Another is a pro-gambling family. So, our arsonist, if it wasn't kids playing with matches, is an equal opportunity firebug."

"I would not know about that, Sheriff."

"No? You seemed a lot more knowledgeable this morning, Miss Tassel. You were telling me my business this morning."

"I am sorry if you got that impression, Sheriff Harrison."

"If I got that impression, is it? You don't have to show off your psychobabble with me, young lady. I know you're one of the educated ones."

Linda felt a rod of steel go up her back. "Sir?"

He exhaled. "Look, Miss Tassel. I'm sorry your friend hasn't showed up yet. And I've made a few inquiries. I'd like to help more, but you see how my day's going. I'm glad you folks got the fire out, but I need to know if it was set purposefully and why." He flipped through a penciled in notebook. "The missing girl's father says the fire destroyed some kind of costume that belonged to her."

"Her Fancy Shawl!"

His eyebrow quirked up. "Was this something of value?"

Linda looked over the Sheriff's head for Tad. Only he would understand the panic clutching at her. Stop. Look at the sheriff. White people wanted eye contact, always. "It was very beautiful," she heard a small version of her voice answer, "with beadwork of maple leaves dancing all over it."

"How much might it go for?"

"Go for?"

"Cost, Miss Tassel."

She centered her gaze between the policeman's eyes. "I cannot even guess. You might ask Dora and Breman Tanner."

"The Atlanta shopkeepers? Have they gotten a good enough look at it?"

"Oh yes. When it was on display in the dance tent."

Her thoughts rushed in as Sheriff Harrison scribbled in his notebook. Why wasn't Rising Fawn's shawl still in the dance tent? Even the clothes of her friend were disappearing. Would there soon be no trace of Rising Fawn?

The sheriff was writing. Was she implicating these people in an arson investigation because she didn't like the prices they put on everything?

Linda felt the weight of the day on her shoulders.

"Thank you, Miss Tassel. You ought to get some rest now." Sheriff Harrison gestured to Tad, who was already on his way over. "Take your girl to her folks, son. I have a few more questions for you. Alone."

Chapter Seventeen

Tad didn't like leaving Linda, but she was safe here, he kept telling himself. As he stood before her family's tent, he put his sooty graduation present, his Fossil watch, on her slim wrist. It looked nice there, the gold stars and rising moon, the hands and numbers glowing in the dark. Tad imagined it protecting her.

"I've set the alarm for twelve forty-five," he told her. "Plenty of time for you to get to the demonstration tent by one o'clock."

"Two hours."

"Yeah. Two hours rest for us both. Then we take up the search, right?"

"Right."

"We'll find her, Linda."

"Keep saying that."

He wrapped her in his arms and kissed her forehead before she went inside the family's tent.

Outside, Linda's grandmother was perched on a low stool by the campfire. "All the families are together again," Delores Longknife said, taking Tad's hand.

He looked down at her bifocal eyeglasses, her dark, intelligent eyes

155

magnified in the lenses. "Yes, ma'am. That's good."

She squeezed his hand lightly, then went back to working her stitches into Linda's Fancy Shawl. The wild roses glistened in the lantern's light.

Tad remembered that Delores Longknife was a self-described owl. She prided herself in keeping night hours past the younger two generations of her family. She had the latest bedtime. Tad wondered if Linda would succeed in slipping past her grandmother in two hours time for their meeting.

"Have you got much more to sew, Mrs. Longknife?" he asked, hoping to sound merely curious.

"Oh, I am just making sure all the beads are secure. Ahyoka will dance stronger and higher and faster than ever tomorrow, if she must dance for herself and Rising Fawn."

"'If?' Does that mean you think Rising Fawn might return for their butterfly dance?"

Dolores Longknife gestured to a spot across from her, where a blanket was set out. It was an invitation to sit. Tad thought of telling her that Sheriff Harrison was waiting to question him, but that would be too impolite to an elder of whom he was very fond. And he wanted to know her thoughts on Rising Fawn's whereabouts. Tad sat.

Mrs. Longknife changed the subject. "Do you think there will be trouble at the Church of the Dove tonight?" she asked.

"Because the Joyce family has to share emergency quarters there with the Reeds? Well, I guess Pastor Tim might have his hands full keeping peace between them."

"Strange, the fire starting at those two campsites."

"Yeah. And Linda is pretty broken up about Rising Fawn's belongings being burned. Especially her dancing shawl."

"I walked the ashes of the Reed campsite, Tad, right after the fire folks were finished. Thought I could find something of Rising Fawn's shawl...a remnant or a few beads that I could sew into Linda's shawl for the dance tomorrow."

"What did you find?"

"Other things made of glass—shattered bottles, earrings belonging to Peggy Reed. Tad, I know that shawl. I knew the colors to look for, shining up in the moon's light."

"Do you think the shawl wasn't burnt? Maybe wasn't even there?"

"Yes. That is what I think."

"Somebody took it away? Before the fire?"

"Maybe."

"Any idea who?"

"That I will leave to you and my granddaughter. Such thoughts poison my mind."

Tad sighed. "I know what you mean, ma'am."

Tad watched her pulling her needle and thread in, out. It soothed his worry.

In the distance, he heard Guli and the softball players pitching to each other on a field illuminated by a string of light bulbs. If he wandered over, would they ask him to join them?

"Go, play," Dolores Longknife urged him.

"I need to talk to the sheriff now, ma'am."

"After, then. And share the sweat house and swim with the ballplayers, too."

"You think they'd allow it?"

"I have already told them to allow it." She reached under her stool and pulled out a worn-to-perfection baseball mitt. His own. She held it out to him. "Play."

"All right. I will."

He stood, tucking the glove under his arm, feeling renewed.

"And, Tad?"

"Ma'am?"

"All will be better tomorrow, I think."

Chapter Eighteen

Linda turned over, restless. She could no longer hear the fragments of conversation between Tad and her grandmother outside the tent. He'd gone on to answer Sheriff Harrison's questions, then on to play softball, she hoped.

Had her grandmother remembered to give him his glove? The one Guli had carefully oiled, then wrapped around a softball and tied, so that it would be ready to catch a larger ball than it was used to? Maybe she should get up, to make sure. No, sleep, she told herself. Her grandmother had not forgotten.

Guli would welcome Tad, and take him to the sweat house to sit with the other ball players, before they would jump into the cold water of the creek's swimming hole. They would tease Tad about the color of his skin, call him Ghostwalker or He Frightens Game. Her Tad would not mind when they did this. And they would respect him for his good nature.

When she and Tad met deep in the night he would be refreshed and whole and beautiful, cleansed by the fire and the water. He would be ready to help her puzzle out what to do to bring Rising Fawn home.

Linda listened. She could hear her grandfather near the door of the tent, lightly snoring. It would subside into a low rumble once her owl grandmother joined him.

Linda listened to the western side of the tent, to her parents' intertwined breathing. She remembered that sound from her earliest days— the separate, winding strands. It reminded her of the necklace that Jim Greene had given Rising Fawn, its silver strands weaving around each other to make a perfect shape, a circle. Would she and Tad ever breathe like that?

Close beside her parents' place, Aunt Theda's soft snore came from her water mattress. The mattress cooled and massaged the limbs that no longer had the ability to keep her standing. The water mattress eased her night, Aunt Theda said. It had given her back her dreams.

Who else wanted her dreams back? Shirley Cutcheon. Linda's eyes misted with sorrow when she thought of Shirley, so fragile and sad. She was wounded in spirit worse than her aunt was in body. Doctors did not have a cure for Shirley's grief, or for a brother so protective that he sought to bury her up in his mountain home. No. Not bury. What was she thinking?

She should not be thinking at all. Linda chastised her mind's wanderings. She should be sleeping, or she would not be rested when the moon was high and it was time to meet Tad. She must put herself to sleep, resting one section at a time. She began with her overcrowded mind, concentrating on her head, sending it down into her pillow's depths. By the time she got to her shoulder, the coming sleep was so delicious that she felt herself smile.

Then another pillow came, hard and clumsy, over her face.

Linda screamed into it, but heard no sound, not even after her deep, panicked gulps of sweet-smelling air that her desperate lungs drew in. Mama! Daddy! Grandfather! Aunt Theda! Her mind called out their names even as her struggling limbs melted.

Grandmother, outside, sewing my shawl, hear me!

Linda saw Delores Longknife then, suddenly. Her face took on a stricken look for a moment. She shook her head, and went back to her sewing, singing softly to drive away unwanted night spirits. I am no spirit, Grandmother, Linda cried out. Come help me before I am gone, disappeared!

But she went on with her sewing.

Only thought, no sound came from her, Linda realized as she walked around her grandmother. Her footsteps made no impression on the ground. She ran around the tent in time to see a broad form emerge from under it. He dragged a girl behind him, then lifted her over his shoulder. The girl's hair hung down the man's back, a shower of black.

Linda pounded on the man's shoulder. "Put her down!" she demanded. The man ignored her. He shifted his burden slightly. When he did, the girl's face turned sideways. It was illuminated in the moonlight.

Her cry to the inert girl stayed lodged in her throat. Blackness descended, but not before Linda saw that the girl's face was her own.

Chapter Nineteen

Tad approached the tent where Guli and Linda had performed that day. Could Swimmer Reed have remembered incorrectly about removing his daughter's shawl from the display table? Or maybe he'd put it somewhere else on purpose? Why? To garner more sympathy and votes for his anti-gambling stance? Or was this too wild a speculation? He missed having Linda dissect the ramblings of his mind.

Maybe he should slip into the tent and look for clues. Or did he just want to delay his meeting with Sheriff Harrison? No, he owed it to Dolores Longknife, who had patiently sifted through the ashes of the Reed campsite. He redirected his steps.

As he approached, Tad saw a moonlit shadow on the tent wall. He stopped. The shadow disappeared. Tad waited. Nothing. He walked on. He heard a scurrying. A smell, now—the metallic smell of fear.

"Hey, wait!" Tad called out to the figure's hunched moving shadow. He caught up, grabbed the denim shirt, turned him around.

It was Bill Chasteen.

The brown paper wrapped bundle he was carrying dropped to his feet. Tad saw the gleaming beadwork of a red maple leaf through the tear in the paper.

"Where did you get that, Mr. Chasteen?" he asked.

"Get it? I rescued it from the flames. I deserve something—a reward, don't I?"

"I'm sure Sheriff Harrison would be interested in the story of your rescue."

"But—"

"He's waiting for me at the church." Tad took his burden from his arms. "Let's go."

The wiry man walked meekly beside him, for which Tad was grateful.

As the church came into view, Tad saw Dora and Breman Tanner talking with Sheriff Tanner outside its doors. They rushed toward him.

"The sheriff was about to send a posse out looking for you, Tad," Dora cried. "We were just telling him that, in the absence of your parents, we would take it upon ourselves to be sure your rights were not violated. Oh, my! What have you there?"

Tad's civil liberties disappeared once her sights fell on the package. "It's Rising Fawn's shawl."

"He tried to steal it!" Bill Chasteen found his voice. "He's in with those two, Sheriff, thick as thieves. They sent him for it, but I

164

got there first. I want that money, I need that money to rebuild my house!"

Tad's head swam. "I found him, in the shadows, hiding the shawl. He was running away."

Dora Tanner's voice was hesitant because of her sniffles. "We would not engage in arson to procure a little Indian beadwork we'd admired. How could anyone think such a thing?"

Her husband took her in a protective hold. "Sheriff Harrison, we are respected members of the Atlanta business community!" he said in an outraged voice.

Pastor Tim opened the church's doors. He was followed out by a gaggle of both Reed and Joyce children, followed by their arguing parents. "Bill!" he called out over the din, "Come inside. You're overdue for your medication."

Sheriff Harrison shook his head.

Tad shifted his weight where he sat in the uncomfortable wooden bench set up against the outside wall of the Church of the Dove. He was so tired he couldn't think straight. When was Sheriff Harrison going to listen to his side of the story? He was clearly last on his list. The sheriff was getting back at his own foot-dragging to their appointed meeting, he figured.

Tad looked down at his wrist, then remembered that he'd given his watch to

Linda. It was eleven-thirty when he'd left her at her family's tent. He had time. They would meet when this was over.

Inside the church, the war between the Reed and Joyce families had died down. Sheriff Harrisons interrogations about Rising Fawn's shawl must have begun. It had not been twenty-four hours since it had gone missing. How was he more concerned about the shawl than its wearer?

Surely Pastor Tim would defend him, tell the sheriff about Bill Chasteen's mood swings? The Tanners, as irritating as they were, they would too, wouldn't they? They would tell Sheriff Harrison he was no arsonist.

But why should they? Hadn't he and Linda put them on their list of possible suspects in Rising Fawn's disappearance?

How well did Tad know any of these people? He was a visitor, a guest. The only ones who knew him better were sleeping or playing a ball game he hadn't even been invited to join. Why had he ever come to this shrouded, confusing place?

Tad put his head in his hands. How long would they be? When was it time to tell his side of the story? What was his side of the story?

Tad pulled his baseball glove from his jacket pocket. He saw the softball Guli had lodged there, before wrapping it in a soft leather thong. To mold it to the larger ball's shape. Well. Guli was making sure he would not have an ill-fitting glove handicap. That meant something, didn't it?

Tad tucked the glove under his harm, catching its familiar scent. He leaned his head against the white clapboard side of the church. he heard the whoops of the softball players in the distance. Maybe he'd have time to join them once Harrison was finished with his interview. Maybe. He felt himself drifting off.

"Tad!"

He bolted up. "Call time, Coach!" he blurted out, while the memory of the dream that prompted his words faded into the night air.

Sheriff Harrison smiled. "That is my intention, son. Go to bed."

"But, sir—"

"I'll get your statement in the morning. I can't fill my notebook with another word after that vagrant's confused, conflicting statements. Classic unreliable witness. But a much more reliable one came forth on the matter of the fire."

"Who?"

"Oh, don't trouble yourself with that. I've got to get my deputies home to their families." He leaned in closer. "I didn't dare ask much of Rhett and Scarlett without their lawyer present. But both sides of the gambling debate have finally settled down. And tomorrow's another day."

"Where is the shawl, sir?"

"Why?"

"I want Linda to know that it's safe."

"It's safe."

"Good. I'll tell her."

"You do that. And don't leave the campground."

Did the sheriff's voice get harder? Well, maybe they were all growing hard and weary.

Tad listened for sounds of the ball game, but heard nothing but an animal squawk, maybe wings flapping. The moon was high. He caught a glimpse of Sheriff Harrison's watch. It was one-thirty.

"Good night, sir," he said, trying not to sound as panicked as he felt. Late. He was late.

As Tad turned down the pine needle strewn path toward the dance tent the thought, pounded with his footsteps. Wait. Be there. Please wait for me, Ahyoka.

He was thinking of her as her Cherokee name and almost smiled, despite his worry. He slowed to a fast walk. Linda didn't run on clock time, especially here, among the Cherokee. She would understand. She would wait for him.

Tad felt his heart pounding when he reached the dance tent. It was dark inside. Even the string of lights surrounding it were out.

He went in anyway. Maybe Linda was watching the stars from the open center space in the roof. He brought his flashlight from his jacket pocket and flicked it on.

"Ahyoka? Linda?" he called, the flashlight's beam passing over the benches. Then he focused his beam on the lip of the raised wooden stage. It caught the sight of her butterfly Fancy Shawl.

His heart stopped.

"No, please," he whispered. Was she lying there, collapsed under her shawl's folds?

Tad ran up the aisle, knocking his shin on two of the benches. He grabbed the shawl and found that it was just that—the shawl, crumpled on the edge of the stage like a discarded costume of a marionette.

Tad swept the shawl into his arms and breathed in Linda's scent. Three uniformed police deputies swept down on him as Sheriff Harrison handcuffed him behind his back.

"I'm afraid our little talk can't wait till morning, Tad," he said.

Chapter Twenty

At first, Linda thought she was ten years old again. She was coming out from under a dark place, with no dreams. She saw her father's face: smiling, but with worried eyes. He was calling her back to the world. "Linda?" he had said gently. "It's all finished. We can go home."

Her fingers reached for her mouth. But it was not filled with cotton soaking up the blood left by extracted teeth, to make way for her braces. No, it was just her mouth, feeling dry and thirsty.

"Daddy?" she tried to call back her father's face.

"Shhh," a voice hushed her softly. A deep voice. A voice that had forgotten how to be happy. She knew that voice, didn't she?

It was hot. They were moving. Linda could only see grayness. Gray and scratchy. Burlap? What was wrong with her eyes, that they could only see this dim world?

Then it came back—the pillow, the sweet smell of ether, the struggle. Had she left her body and viewed what was happening to her from the outside. Or was that a dream? No matter. She was inside her body now, and it was stiff and being knocked about.

She tried to piece together the clues of this journey over rough roads. The roar of the engine sounded like a truck. Almost everyone at the festival had a pickup truck, so that didn't narrow things down much. Her limbs weren't tied but she was inside a sack of that scratchy burlap. Both her legs felt dead. No, not dead, she realized slowly: asleep, because the way they'd been lying.

Good, then. Her first task was clear—to bring feeling back into her legs. Then, when her chance came, she could run. Run where? To Tad. Tad would come looking for her. Was it past their appointed meeting time? Linda remembered Tad's watch. Slowly, she lifted her arm so she could see the its glowing dial at her wrist, there in the dark. Ten minutes past two o'clock. Could that be right? Of course it was right, Tad was very exact. He was going to help her get better at being on time, at looking at clocks and watches when they attended Morris University together in the Fall.

When she did not appear for their meeting, he would worry. Then he would track her, wouldn't he?

The thought didn't give Linda any peace. The more she thought about Tad and what they'd already done in their search for the truth of Rising Fawn's disappearance, the more she imagined that the one who had taken her had found a way to stop him already. That thought made her feel cold and frightened.

Linda reached down, slowly massaging her shins back to life. The tiny stabbings of a thousand pins and needles hurt so much that tears spilled from her cheeks. No crying, she reminded herself, make no sound. Be ready, when the time is right, to run.

Chapter Twenty-one

Tad's mind shut down against the feeling of the handcuffs linking his wrists together behind his back. Sheriff Harrison read him his rights mechanically, without looking at him. That made it seem even more unreal. This is a trap, kept hammering inside Tad's head.

What had the sheriff said? A witness. Not mixed-up, addled, Bill Chasteen, but a credible witness came forth to make everything clear. Who was it? He was the one who set the trap, made Tad look like a fire-starting thief. Who would do that? Why?

Whoever took Rising Fawn. He and Linda were somehow getting close to discovering that person. Where was Linda? And Guli? Rising fawn's abductor couldn't be framing them all at once.

"If you cannot afford a lawyer, one will be appointed for you before any questioning if you wish. If you decide to answer questions now—"

There was a rush at Tad's ears. No, it was not his confused brain blocking out the words. The sound was confusing the deputies, too. And it was bloodcurdling. Tad saw his chance as they all turned toward it. He bolted for the woods. The sound got louder. He kept running. Almost there. Behind him, were they raising their guns? He had to get into that misty darkness. He had to find Linda.

Someone tackled him, brought him down. The injury Mitch Ryder's fist had caused opened up, spattering a rock with blood.

"Aw, don't do this, kid," a deputy said uneasily, breathing hard as he pulled Tad to his feet. "Things are spooked enough around here."

Dust joined the screams now. "What the—?" The deputy released his hold an instant before a barreling shoulder came out of the dust and landed in Tad's middle, doubling him over. Then his feet lifted off the ground. He opened his mouth and chocked on the dust. He was not feeling at all well.

"It's a good thing you're light on those heron legs, Buffalo Man."

Guli shined a flashlight in Tad's eyes, then checked under a cool cloth pressed against his bleeding lip.

Tad managed a feeble groan.

"Can't stay here long. They follow pretty well, for Anglos."

"Where are we going?" Tad heard his own voice ask. It sounded like he'd been gargling with gravel.

"Higher. Into the deep woods. Don't worry. These are Cherokee hills. They hid a thousand of us from the federal soldiers back in the time of the Trail of Tears."

"But I can't hide. Linda—"

"Shhh," Guli cautioned. "An Anglo doctor would stitch that lip of yours. Here, plantain leaves will heal it without a scar."

"Really?"

"If you don't talk so much. Don't want to become more ugly than you already are."

Tad grunted as Guli removed the wad of cloth. He checked under the leaves, then pressed them back against the wound. "One more soak in the spring for this," he decided of the cloth. "Then, we climb higher."

Tad watched Guli slip away noiselessly. There were streaks of red running down the back of his sweatshirt. His blood? Is that why the world went fuzzy? Tad felt the police cuffs still anchoring his hands behind his back, the strain they were putting at his shoulders.

Guli returned and cooled Tad's lip. "Now let's get you upright, with cuffs in front."

How was he going to do that? "Are you crazy?"

"No. Are you double joined?"

No!"

"You can still do it."

"Do what?"

"Stretch. Arms. You barely have a rear to get past, you can do it. Sit. Then one leg at a time, through those arms. Simple."

It wasn't. But with Guli's patient coaxing, and a few grunts of frustration, Tad managed. It felt much better with his arms in front of him, even if his wrists were still clasped.

Guli looked over a ridge. "Let's go," he said. I have lost sight of their lights."

"Lights?"

"We will spot them again at Second Heaven. Can you walk?"

"Sure." He only stumbled once in getting to his feet.

They climbed through the undergrowth of rhododendron. Tad realized they were on a less-trodden track up than the one he and Linda had taken.

"Guli?"

"What is it?"

"I was being arrested."

He snorted. "Yes. The cuffs were a dead giveaway."

"You're going to get into trouble for helping me."

"Nobody is helping you. The ball team was coming into camp after our sweat and cold bath in the river. Maybe you were in our way, then got caught in our stampede.

Didn't even see you there on my shoulder until we were halfway up the mountain. Could not leave you to be eaten by a bobcat there, could I?"

"Linda must be wondering—"

"Linda's gone."

"What?"

"Taken. There were drag marks, outside her tent."

"We've got to go back! He's got her."

"Who has got her?"

"The same one who took Rising Fawn. He framed me, to get attention off him. Did the Tanners say I stole the shawls? Started the fire? He's down there!"

"No. They are searching for Ahyoka, down there. That's why I was looking for you."

"Well, you got me. Now what are you going to do with me?"

"For now, get those handcuffs off. I will find a rock big enough, and aim high enough..."

Tad winced. "And accurate. Accurate enough."

Chapter Twenty-two

The rumbling stopped. Linda heard a door slam, then the one on her side opened. She kept her body limp and her eyes closed, even within her grey world, as the arms reached in and picked her up.

They traveled a few steps. Count them, Linda told herself. The counting kept her calm, her breathing even. Twenty-two steps, along a path that was clear of plants or obstruction.

She was placed down on something flat, hard, cool. A rock. It reminded Linda of the stone bier she'd worked to uncover at the Mound Builders' dig site. She thought of the skeleton she'd patiently unearthed there. She had become friends with the thousand- year-old craftswoman, buried with her pie stem carvings all around her. Linda found herself praying to that friend now, for the strength to endure.

The scratchy grey eased away from her face. Linda longed to breath deeper into the cool, pinewoods-scented night air. But she didn't dare. She had to play possum, and not open her eyes. She felt a hand support her neck, gently. Open your senses and take notes, Linda told herself, to fight the fear of being under the control of those hands.

They were large, strong hands. Hands that could snap her neck in seconds. They had calloused fingers. Were Breman Tanner's fingers calloused? He was a city man. His job would probably not cause them. But maybe he worked hard at a sport, or home projects.

Linda remembered Swimmer Reed's callouses, and Bill Chasteen's firewood-chopping hands. What about William Joyce? She could not remember. But he was big enough to carry her with ease. They were all big enough to do that. Sorry, Tad. I am not narrowing down our suspects, she thought.

Fingers drew her hair off her brow. She smelled traces of that sweet vapor that had overcome her. They turned her stomach. Did he have more? Of course he did, and would use it again if she stirred. Linda fought the panic rising like a bitter bile in her throat.

Then he left her side.

Was he worried, or suspicious because she was not waking up?

She had to leave something of herself here, where Tad could find it. She's been sleeping in her sweatshirt and pants, of a soft cotton that would not rip easily. She was barefooted, and no tokens, except...

Tad's watch.

Her mind raced. Tad's wonderful stars and moon watch had been set to beep at the time for them to meet. Had her captor turned it off? It didn't matter, he'd left it on her wrist. Now it must help Tad find her. Where was her captor? She had to calm down, figure out how to get the watch off. She had to leave it for him to find it. She was lying on her side. She opened one eye, the one closest to the rock. The world was dark. Her captor was sitting, back to her, shoulders hunched, about ten feet away. She opened both eyes, now that she knew he was not watching her. Then she knew where she was. Second Heaven.

Linda fought back tears. Thoughts of her time here during her childhood and more recently with Tad came flooding into her mind. Stop that. Get the watch off your wrist. Cry later.

Quietly, patiently, Linda worked the watch free. She caught it before it fell.

She had sat on this rock with Rising Fawn when they were little girls. Along the surface there were small fissures, where they would leave each other notes and small treasures. If only she could find one of them, and leave the watch for Tad to find.

But the surface within easy reach was smooth, with no hiding spots. Her captor rose. Linda narrowed her eyes to slits. Her cold sweat made the watch slip from her grasp. Its numbers, hour and minute, had glowed in the dark. If she dropped the watch in plain sight, the man would find it, she was sure. But he was coming. What else could she do?

The man approached, his face down and bathed in shadows. Linda closed her eyes. His footsteps told her he came closer. Closer. Linda turned the glowing face on the watch over, then let go as she stretched her legs and moaned to cover the sound of it sliding down the rock. She felt her captor lean over and cover her face and head with the sack again.

He did not put her over his shoulder, but carried her like a father carries a child in his arms. He stumbled. Linda heard glass breaking. She tried to keep her body lifeless, but reflexively, she groped for stability. He recovered her with a soft expletive. His voice. She knew it.

He kicked away the remains of Tad's watch before laying her on her side. Stay still, she commanded her shaking limbs. Maybe he will think your mad grab at the air was just that, a startled reflex from an unconscious mind. But she caught the sweet scent of ether, strong again. No. She did not want to go back into that dark place.

Her hands flew out, fingers desperately scratching at the burlap around her face. The calloused fingers caught one wrist and held it tight against her ribcage.

With her other hand, Linda hit something, hard. The sweet liquid spilled. Into the burlap, down her sweatshirt. The man groaned now, before he whacked the side of her head. Not hard. Restrained violence, just enough to stun her into inaction. It worked. He had both her hands in his grip now.

"Don't," Linda pleaded with him.

"Shhh," he answered, as he held the soaked sweatshirt over her face.

She would not breathe. She did not have to breathe. The fumes were in the air, she would outlast them. He began to weave. Yes, they were getting to him, too. His grip would weaken, she would break free, run down the road, find a phone and— Linda felt a hard thrust at her middle. Now she had to breathe. And—what? Find Tad, find Guli, were her final thoughts as she gasped in the awful air.

Chapter Twenty-three

Guli stopped suddenly. Tad, climbing behind him, came to a halt. He was still cuffed. Guli's attempts to free him had only led to a couple of bruises and a cut across Tad's thumb. Guess it was not as easy as in the movies.

"Why did you stop?" he called up.

"Hissst!" Guli grabbed the rock battered chain between the handcuffs and hauled Tad up the rock face to his level. "Look," he said softly. "I think there might be some answers at Second Heaven."

Tad peered over Guli's shoulder and saw a man in black leather pacing the length of a flat rock, yanking his hand through his dark hair. Then he laid a burlap sack down.

"Stay, Guli warned, before going on alone. "Jim Greene?" he called out softly. The two men shook hands. "Come out," Guli then called back to Tad.

Jim Greene's lanky form tensed when stared at Tad's handcuffs. "You guys on the run?" he asked uneasily.

"Yeah. You?"

"I didn't think so until I got home to my trailer. My neighbor Helen told me that half of Roaring Rock's been looking for me. Including the sheriff's department."

"She's a nice lady," Tad said.

"Yeah. Well, at Harmony they said everybody was thinking I took Rising Fawn with me to Maryville. Well, I knew what her daddy would think of that opinion, so I figured this wouldn't be the best time to make my appearance at the festival with my offering of the local delicacy." He leaned down, opening his burlap sack so that Tad and Guli saw the bounty of ramps from Tennessee. "Figured I'd better think all this out here at Seventh Heaven," he finished.

"Rising Fawn did not go with you, then?" Guli asked.

"No. We parted company when they were still setting up for the festival. Rising Fawn was upset with me about going to Maryville for the job interview. We planned to go to Harmony together this year. She was excited about me meeting her friend Ahyoka, and Ahyoka's—wait, that's you, isn't it? Ahyoka's friend from Atlanta?"

"Yeah. Tad Gist."

Jim grinned. "I feel like I know you, man."

Guli rolled his eyes and sighed.

"We've got a terrible thing in common now," Tad said. "Both Ahyoka and Rising Fawn have been taken."

184

Jim ran his hand through his hair again. "What's going on around here, Guli?"

Linda's clan brother heaved a mournful sigh.

Tad touched his lip where it was starting to itch around the plantain leaf. "Wish we knew," he said.

Jim took his shoulder. "Come on over to my bike. I've got some tools in my gear to get those cuffs off. That much we can figure out."

Tad smiled, feeling the first spark of hope since the handcuffs went on. He was glad he had never fought against Linda's feelings about Jim Greene's innocence, as likely a suspect he seemed to everyone else. Now the guy was aiding and abetting his escape without a second thought.

Jim rummaged through the tool compartment under the seat of his mid-level Yamaha ® and pulled out a screwdriver. "Phillip's head. Add a rock and we should be in business," he said, as if the three of them were about to work on a backyard project.

As Guli searched for a heavy rock and Tad tried to keep his already bruised hands out of their way, Jim Greene told his story.

"I promised Rising Fawn that I wouldn't make any decision yet if I was offered a job. And I told her I'd be back for the Butterfly Dance. That's why I drove over those mountains on paved roads. I don't like paved roads and neither does the bike. She's dual-purpose, but we like back roads, generally. I about ruined both tires tearing over from Tennessee to be here before dawn, and now I've blown out the front one."

He placed his screwdriver against an already battered link in the handcuffs. Tad winced while Guli came down on the screwdriver's head with a rock.

His third try worked. Tad was released.

"There!" Jim proclaimed. "We can free jailbirds pretty good, can't we, Guli?"

Linda's clan brother frowned. "I softened it up for you first."

Tad was so glad to have control of his hands again that he didn't mind that he was left with telltale bracelets.

"Well, fugitives of the law, where are we off to now?" Jim asked.

"Higher," Guli said.

"My bike won't go any higher."

"Leave it. We have got to get—"

"Hey," Tad called them over. "Look at this."

"Want a souvenir of your daring escape?" Guli chided.

"I thought I saw something glowing."

"A firefly maybe, city boy."

Tad dropped to his knees. "It's a moon."

"Moon?"

"Yeah. And here's the sun. My sun, stars. Scattered. Broken and scattered, but they're here."

Jim came closer. "Tad, what are you talking about?"

"My watch. Parts of my watch."

Chapter Twenty-Four

She was not moving. That's what Linda realized at first. Then that the dense blackness began to lift. She swung out her hands wild-ly.

"Ahyoka."

A voice in the darkness. She was not alone. "Rising Fawn?"

"Keep looking toward my voice, you will see me."

The outline of her friend's face came first, then her features. Linda pulled her friend close and the girls hugged each other.

"I am not buried? He has not buried us alive?"

"No, no. That is what I thought at first too. Oh, Ahyoka, I am so sorry."

Linda laughed out her relief. "I am so glad you're alive."

"But I asked for you. I said I could not do it without you. Forgive me, Ahyoka. I was afraid, and I thought someone would catch him before he took you, too."

Linda stroked her friend's hair. "That was good thinking. I'm happy you did that.

Help is coming now. Help is right behind me."

There were only remnants of the sweet smell that had taken her into oblivion a second time. Linda realized that her sweatshirt had been replaced by a soft cotton blouse. She sat up and felt sick. Someone else's scent. Someone else's scent in the blouse. The man's scent. She was shaking.

Rising Fawn held her arms. "He threw the blouse in here. He did not touch you in that way. I put it on you. Don't cry, Ahyoka, you are all right."

"And you? Did he hurt you, Rising Fawn?"

"No. I was afraid of that at first. Because he gave me juice that made me sleep when I cried out. But I checked myself carefully. And he promised to stop making me drink if I stayed quiet. And I did, and he has.

"I don't think he's a bad man, Ahyoka. At first I thought my father hired him to keep me here. My father is so angry with me. But this man has lost his way, and he had to keep covering his tracks once he took me. He is so out of balance."

"Who is he?"

"Didn't you see him?"

"No. Who is he? What does he want of us?"

A glare of light invaded their darkness. Linda's eyes kept blinking, taking in shelves, depleted winter staples—potatoes, onions, hanging herbs. It was a root cellar, she realized. They were being kept underground. The powerful flashlight's beam shining in her face made it impossible to see the man standing beside an opened storm door. Two packages, carefully wrapped in brown paper, fell to the floor. Then the girls were enveloped in darkness again.

Linda fought back a wave of nausea. She leaned back against an earth wall and closed her eyes. She heard Rising Fawn unfold he paper, then the rustle of fabric.

"Ahyoka! I feel the raised beadwork—the pink rose pattern your grandmother learned from the Seneca clan mother at last Harmony Festival. These are our Fancy Shawls, yours and mine."

The door opened again, the light blinding them.

"Do not wear them yet," the voice came, finally speaking a whole sentence. "You need the harsh medicine. You need to be purified first."

Linda stood, leaning on Rising Fawn's arm. She finally recognized the voice.

Chapter Twenty-five

Tad pressed the strap of his watch to his face. "Linda was here!" he shouted. "I gave her my watch."

His enthusiasm faded as he took in the expressions on the other guys' faces. Of course. She wouldn't have broken his graduation present. Someone else had smashed it. What had that person done to Linda?

Jim Greene's flashlight swept the area. "I'll look for tracks," he said quietly.

Tad gathered the watch's fragments in his hands, willing them back together, willing them to talk, to tell them where Linda was.

He felt Guli's hand at his shoulder and shrugged it off. "She is all right. I would know it if she wasn't. Jim would know about Rising Fawn."

"Maybe," Guli said.

"Not maybe. We would know."

"Ahyoka is my clan sister. I respect your vision, and hope it is a true one. But we Cherokee are not such absolute people."

They heard a sound in the bushes beyond. Guli took hold of Tad's sleeve to

191

silence their conversation. From the undergrowth, a goat wandered onto the flat stone.

Both of them breathed out together.

"One of Ned Socowah's," Tad said, approaching the animal. "Linda and I saw it pegged down outside the cabin when we brought up their dinners. I recognize him by his injured leg."

Guli patted the shaggy head. "Her leg, city boy," he said, kneeling before the obviously female utters. "And there is nothing wrong with her leg."

"But Ned said—"

"Look. Recently shaved, but no injury beneath, no scar or an old wound, or rash. Recently shaved. For new dance leggings, maybe."

"Ned lied."

"Maybe you misunderstood."

"I remember it clearly. I even remember thinking it was odd that he was being so chatty. Not like the guy, you know?"

"He is not very talkative."

"Listen. Do dancers replace the leggings one at a time?"

"No. Usually both together."

"Then why was only one leg of the goat shaved?"

"I don't know."

"And why did Ned lie about it?"

Jim Greene returned. "Truck tire marks are fresh. And heading north."

"Overturn one lie, there are twenty behind it," Guli said. "I think we had better return that goat."

"But, aren't the sheriff and his men advancing on us?" Jim asked. "Do we have time to—"

"We make time," Tad said, "for this."

The pre-dawn light eliminated any hope they had of approaching Ned Socowah's cabin unseen.

"Ideas?" Jim asked.

"We return the goat," Guli said, "then ask questions. Polite questions," he warned. "And shove those handcuffs up your sleeve, Buffalo Man."

Tad grinned despite himself, despite his worry. Guli was using Linda's nickname for him. That meant he was finally getting somewhere with her clan brother. He took a hold of the goat's shaggy mane.

A rife shot cracked the early morning air.

The frightened goat bolted away, running in a zigzag line. Tad, Jim and Guli took quick shelter behind a poplar tree.

More shots.

"He's firing above our heads," Guli maintained.

"Oh?" Tad pulled in a ragged breath. "That's a comfort."

"Ideas?" Jim asked again, more urgently this time.

"Let's stay with the first one," Guli persisted. "*Hi gina lii!*" he called out.

They head a few steps across the cabin's porch. "Guli Whitepath?"

"*Ha yu.* Yes, sir. And Tad Gist and Jim Greene. We have brought your goat."

"You should not have. I sent her down the mountain. I sent them all down."

"Why is that, sir?"

"My sister and I are leaving this place."

Guli left the tree's shelter and stood in plain sight. "Do you need help in packing your truck?"

"No. Go away!"

Tad and Jim walked over and stood on either side of Guli in the mist. Tad saw Ned Socowah's rifle resting in the crook of his arm.

"I have a clan sister missing, sir," Guli said now. "We tracked her here. "We think Rising Fawn is with her."

Tad saw Ned Socowah's arms tense. But the rifle stayed in its cradled position. "Ask those two about them!" he shouted, nodding toward Tad and Jim. "No honor. Unmindful of our ways!"

Tad took a step forward and opened his arms. Too late he realized his gesture made him a bigger target. His handcuffs slipped down to his wrists, too. He could feel Guli's exasperated sigh behind him.

"You're right, Mr. Socowah," Tad said. "Jim and I are pretty ignorant of Cherokee ways, but—"

"We came here to bring the girls back to their relatives," Jim finished, now standing beside him.

Ned's shoulders dropped. "But I need them."

Tad looked to Jim, who nodded. "Take us instead," Tad offered.

The morning light was good enough now to see Ned Socowah's features harden. "You cannot do the dance!"

"Dance?" Tad whispered from his dry throat.

"The Butterfly Dance," Guli said softly behind them. "Of course. He wants them to do the Butterfly Dance to bring Shirley out of her grief."

Jim turned in Guli's direction. "Why didn't he just ask them?"

Ned came to the end of his porch. "Because they have contaminated themselves with you two! I listened to them in their motel room after the storm. Taking about their white boyfriends. They were both unfit to do the dance. They needed the harsh medicine of purification first."

Tad felt his knees weaken.

"It is all right," Guli said behind him. It is not as bad as it sounds. No worse than a Christian baptism."

Tad fought the urge to pull the man on the porch down. "Ned Socowah," he called out his anger instead. "Why does our love dishonor these young women? Because it come from white hearts?"

Jim Greene's anger whipped out of his voice, matching Tad's own. "You bring us grief while seeking the healing of your sister!"

Guli gripped both their shoulders. "Easy," he whispered, before releasing them and walking toward the man on the porch. "It is almost dawn *aginalii*," he said. "After the dance, you can take all three of us in exchange for the girls. Agreed?"

Suddenly Ned turned his head like a hawk toward the pines beyond. A harsh, mechanical voice sounded through a bullhorn. "Mr. Socowah, your house is surrounded by sheriff's deputies. Put down your weapon."

A hunted look entered Ned's eyes. He raised the rifle and backed in toward the door.

Tad breathed out. "Oh, no."

"Right," Guli agreed. "If he gets inside we have a siege on our hands. With hostages."

But before he reached the door, it opened. Shirley Cutcheon came out on the porch. She stood tall and unafraid, reminding Tad of her best moments during their visit. But her eyes were angry.

"Get inside!" Ned barked at his sister.

"This must stop, now."

"You do not know what—"

"I know you have frightened my friends. You have pointed death at men who came for them, even at the one who eased my husband off on his sky journey. This is wrong."

"It is for you!"

"No, brother. It is for yourself. Because my sadness reminds you of your own."

Ned looked as if she'd struck him. But he shook her words off. "My sadness is long past."

His sister's voice gentled. "But still part of you. So deep a part that you, the firefighter, have begun to start fires in order to rescue your warrior brothers again and again."

"I did not rescue them! I was pinned under a beam that morning in Beirut! Listening as they screamed and burned. Helpless."

"I know," Shirley said softly. "I hear them too. And I heard Rising Fawn, didn't I? So you gave her my sleeping pills and told me it was the wind. I still hear my husband and your soldier friends, brother."

That's why Linda felt so strange after her conversation with Ned Socowah after their surprise visit, Tad realized. He remembered the man's words 'I only use them when I have to...you understand...I treat her decent...she has to help me.' He was not talking about his sister. He was looking for Linda's permission to drug Rising Fawn with his sister's sleeping pills.

Shirley stepped closer. "We both need the Butterfly Dance, Ned. For the death of our warriors."

She held out her hands and waited.

Ned gave her the rifle.

"They will not do it now," he whispered.

"Yes, we will," Linda said, emerging from the cabin with Rising Fawn beside her. Tad's heart leapt. They looked a little shaken, and their hair was wet, like they'd just come in off the beach, or a swimming hole. Their splendid shawls were wrapped around them.

Tad felt an aching need to hold Linda, to make sure she was safe. But he knew she was when their eyes finally met. The girls stepped off the porch and made a wide stomping circle on the ground.

Sheriff Harrison came out of the woods, with two deputies walking behind him. He took Ned Socowah's rifle from Shirley and handed it to the deputy on his left.

"Is everyone all right here, son?" he asked Tad.

"Appears so, sir," Tad said.

"Might you wait?" Shirley asked the sheriff and his men. "Allow them to do the dance?"

"Mrs. Cutcheon," Sheriff Harrison touched the rim of his hat. "You and these young people just did something that I could not have done with reinforcements from three counties around. You can have all the time you need."

Guli joined the girl's stomped out circle and faced Shirley. "I will sing it," he offered.

Shirley nodded, with tears in her eyes.

Tad and Jim stepped back. The sheriff posted his deputies on either side of Ned and his sister.

Then he approached Tad, pointing to the broken handcuffs. "County property," he said.

"Glad to return them," Tad offered.

"Got you on resisting arrest, too."

"Anything else?"

"Well, since Bill Chasteen had a burst of conscience and told us that Ned Socowah's truck was where he'd rescued the shawl from, and you've been framed as a fire starter, and Ned was not nearly so careful with his second abduction as he was with the first...no."

"Could helping to fight the fire be considered community service, sir, to clear the slate on my transgressions?"

The sheriff scratched the side of his face. "I'll consider it. "Now, as for your friend there," looking at where Guli was stomping out a dancing circle with the girls, "assisting the escape of—"

"Oh, Guli hardly noticed I was on his back until over two thousand feet up."

"Insensitive lout, isn't he?"

"No, sir. I'm just light as a feather."

"I see." The growing, reluctant smile on the man's face faded before he spoke again. "Tad. You and your friends. I had you wrong from the start. I had it all wrong."

"We were wrestling with it as best we could, sir."

Sheriff Harrison put out his hand. Tad took it and tried not to wince when his firm grip squeezed his aching thumb. He didn't succeed.

The man surveyed his bruising fingers. "Say, you're not going to go all Yankee on me and complain about police brutality to your parents, are you?"

"My parents? They're here? You called them?"

"With women disappearing and the county burning up around me? No! But I met them. They said they were here to pick you up after the festival. Don't you remember your own family plans?"

"It's Sunday," Tad realized slowly. "Harmony Festival is over."

Jim Greene joined them. "Not quite. It moved up the mountain." He nodded toward the trees as Cherokee people in their full regalia dress walked through the morning mist and past the sheriff's deputies.

Through the crowd came Tad's parents and Maggie. His sister flew into his arms, then allowed their mother and father to join in her hug.

"Have they started the Butterfly Dance?" his sister whispered at his ear as if they were in church, which he supposed, they were, being between Second and Third Heaven.

"Just in time Sprite," he told her as they took their place on the ground with the other families.

Guli nodded and Ned and Shirley stepped into the dancers' stomp circle. He sat between them and began a low chant, deep and pained, from the back of his throat. Linda and Rising Fawn responded, swirling around their circle in a tight, slow, dance of grief.

Tad noticed that neither Ned or Shirley looked anywhere but the ground at first, deep expressions of pain etched int their faces. Slowly, Shirley reached across Guli to take her brother's hand. In each other's firm grasp, they looked, first at each other, then toward the dancers.

Guli yelped into the next part of his song.

Now anger fed through the music, and the dancers whipped the ground with the long-fringed edges of their shawls. Their tight steps now jutted, stung. Even their turtle shell rattles sounded harsh. Everyone watched, fascinated, as the very scent of the air seemed charged and bitter.

Guli's song changed again, its syllables now seeded with hope. Linda and Rising Fawn's dance slowed, then began to flutter. The shawls unwound out of their tight cocoons. The beads glistened in the early morning light.

"The maple leaves, the roses, so pretty!" Maggie proclaimed from Tad's lap. He kissed the top of her head. Tad knew how much he loved his little sister. He began to understand Ned Socowah's hope for Shirley's recovery, though not how it had twisted into such a nightmare for them all. But the nightmare was over, here, now, on this glorious Sunday morning. Hope had arrived, Tad saw as the dance ended. It was even in the eyes of the young widow and her brother.

Coach Kramer had been right about Stoker Vann. The affable Cherokee sub-chief had one mean fastball. But Tad cracked one of his pitches into left field late in the game for a double. He had that to remember.

Linda's beautiful eyes gazed shyly at the blue embroidery pattern she'd spun through the belt he wore. It signified Tad's place on Guli Whitepath's team. They had lost six to five, even with his RBI double.

Tad had done his best, he could tell Coach Kramer that. Even Guli had shoved his shoulder and said "We will beat them next year."

Linda wore the red sundress that was his favorite. Her shoulders were draped in a lacy black shawl whose fringed ends were secured by glistening, sky blue beads.

"Do you think our dance had any effect, Tad?" she asked him quietly once they were finally alone together after the game.

"Yes. I think it was a start back for Ned. He caused a lot of misery, but Sheriff Harrison knows it came from a damaged part of him."

"It could have been worse," she whispered, but even as she shrugged, her shoulders shook, her voice quivered, as it had a few times during the day. Tad took her into his arms.

"*Wa to*, Taddeusz," she whispered. "Rising Fawn and I have good taste."

"In white men?"

"In men."

"What do you think will happen between Rising Fawn and Jim Greene?"

"I think it is good that Jim came back, with or without finding ramps for her mother. And I think even Swimmer Reed was impressed by his willingness to sacrifice his freedom for hers. I am grateful for your courage too, Tad."

He held her closer. "If Shirley hadn't come out of that doorway, if Sheriff Harrison and his men had not been patient, holding their fire, if you and Rising Fawn hadn't danced— "

"But it all happened as it should have," Linda said before she reached up and kissed him beside the damaged part of his lip. "Maybe the Harmony Festival will achieve some harmony after all."

"Better late than never," Tad agreed.

Linda pulled out a chestnut-colored corduroy jacket from a bag at her feet. It had red beadwork pattern of a pair of cardinals sewn into its wide lapels. She held it up to Tad's chest. "Like it?"

"Sure."

"I know the jacket's style is old. I got it at a thrift store. But I tried to make it fancy with the beads. Try it on."

Tad obliged. The arms were too long, but otherwise it was a perfect fit. He loved that she knew him that well. And the beadwork was spectacular. She was a good student of her grandmother.

Linda brushed off his shoulders. "Yes. A punched-out ball player, but a well dressed one. Now we can sing."

"Sing?"

"The final event at Harmony Festival," she told him as they emerged, hand in hand, from the tent to join their families.

"We join Pastor Tim at the church and sing 'I'll Fly Away,' together."

"In whose language?"

"Both."

Tad looked over a smiling, intertwined jumble of young and old Cherokee, Irish, Scot, Polish and many other culture-mixed Americans in diverse versions of their Sunday-best clothes.

"Both," he said. "Of course."

The End

Readers we need you.

Please leave a review, even a one liner counts, and has a big influence on our future sales.

Eileen Charbonneau

books

also published by BWL

Publishing Inc.

Young Adult

Death at Little Mound

American Civil War Brides

Seven Aprils

Mercies of the Fallen

Ursula's Inheritance

The Code Talker Chronicles

Book 1: I'll Be Seeing You
Book2: Watch Over Me

2020 Bestselling Author
Eileen Charbonneau

Eileen Charbonneau's stories explore the perspectives of people often left out of history: women, first peoples, immigrants, and the marginalized in her fiction. She lives in the brave little state of Vermont with her husband. She adores him, her kids and grandchild. Eileen loves reading, attending good plays and movies, exploring her state, country and world. Oh, and Vermont maple creemies. (Write to her at eileencharbonneau@gmail.com and she'll tell you what they are!)

You can find her at:

https://bookswelove.net/charbonneau-eileen/
eileencharbonneau.com
email: eileencharbonneau@gmail.com
twitter: @EileenC1988
Facebook: Eileen Charbonneau Author
Instagram: eileencharbonneau

Blogs: http://manituwak.blogspot.com
https://bwlauthors.blogspot.com

BWL Publishing

bwlpublishing.ca